To Deba
Enjoy
with your wonderful feeling
Harry D

Alita's Sacred Journey

A Native's Mystical Journey to Help
Alleviate Her Auntie's and Uncle's Suffering

Harold S. Derbitsky

PublishAmerica
Baltimore

ISBN: 1-60474-279-8 (softcover)
ISBN: 978-1-4489-4870-3 (hardcover)
PUBLISHED BY PUBLISHAMERICA, LLLP
www.publishamerica.com
Baltimore

Printed in the United States of America

The Author's Perspective

I am proud of my Native name—Standing Elk. I have been privileged to work and/or be involved with numerous Native organizations, ceremonies and/or communities for the past twenty years and I believe some of my understanding of the Native world is rooted in this book. *However, I was not born as a Native, and do not pretend to fully understand what it is to think or live, in this world, as an Aboriginal person.* Obviously, I have heard the stories and travesties of justice regarding the Native plight of residential schools, colonization, being classified as a 'savage', and 'white people' pretending they know what is best for the Native People. Whenever, I hear these stories, it touches my heart, evokes my compassion and makes me aware that I have not lived these stories; that I have simply heard the 'crying and prayers of a nation' as an outsider.

Therefore, the *primary focus* of this book is to introduce my readers to something quite extraordinary, outside of the realm of being Native.

Early in the 1990's the Native psyche and the sufferings of the Native People moved me. Their understanding of 'Spiritual' was powerful, but this did not seem to alleviate the constant suffering of the People. In 'Alita's Journey to Truth—The Early Years', I approached this previous book as an introduction to the answer to the suffering of the Native People, and it was mostly targeted to their minds.

In this book, this is not true, *it is written for the general public.* However, I have been drawn to the conclusion more and more that the same lack of understanding in the present day Indian or Native world is the same as is in today's global world. Both 'status quo' worlds, Native and Non-Native, pretend they know answers about self-esteem, mental health problems and/or addictions; yet upon deeper investigation, this has proved to be false. However, at the leading edge of both these worlds, I have come to recognize the existence of 'pockets of profound wisdom'; a wisdom that is pure and sacred.

It is my intention that this gentle and entertaining book will provide a few clues to assist in alleviating the suffering of people of all walks of life.

To my readers, I say thank-you. I appreciate all that undertake Alita's Journey, for in my heart I know they will be enriched.

"Mitakuye oyasin (Lakota)

We are all related. All are welcome here."

That is my belief and the story of **All My Relations**.

Thank You by the Author

In many ways this is an unusual book; every reader who likes it has been attracted to it for different reasons.

Some are drawn to the Native Alita and her understanding of Native mythology and ceremony. Others who experience specific problems such as loneliness and grief or the death of a loved one; this book has helped them to understand the healing power that lies profoundly within each human being. Some have been attracted to Alita's wisdom, which is often far greater than the general level of professional advice given in today's world, while others have been attracted to Alita's love relationships. Some have read the book because they have liked what I have said either professionally or socially.

I must give a personal thanks and tribute to the deceased Sydney Banks[1,2], theosopher, writer, teacher and discoverer of the Three Spiritual Principles, for being the wisest influence in my life. I heartily endorse all his books, CD's, tapes, videos and his website—www.sydneybanks.org. However, this book does not, in any way, reflect the in-depth teachings of Sydney Banks. This can only be discovered by exposing yourself to his material.

I thank Everley Pritchard for her devoted editing and proofreading for the first two sections, and Paul Frizell for the third section. Without them, this book would not be as clear in its communication and expression of ideas. It has been a treat to share our moments together in the pursuit of improving this book.

In the end, I wrote this book to alleviate some of my own suffering, and to share a mystical journey with Alita, one which will begin to reveal the magic and wisdom of life, as I understood it, at the moment I wrote these passages.

HAVE A GREAT JOURNEY !!

Table of Contents

Section 3: Alita's Dream

Story of the Three Spirits

Alita's six-year-old niece was sitting on her lap; her big brown eyes eagerly looking into Alita's wise twinkling ones. The little girl pleads, *"Auntie, please tell me your favorite story."*

Alita began:

"This is an old Algonquin story told by a very wise Elder.

Many, many years ago there were three Gods or Spirits living with the People. The Spirits had to make a big journey, far far away. This they were happy about, but they did not know what to do with their Special Powers, which were a gift from the Great Spirit. They had to leave their Powers behind, and this worried them because the People were not in a good place (dissatisfied, selfish and confused).

Then, the First Spirit said, "I know, I know where to leave our Powers. Let us leave them at the top of the highest mountain."

"No," the others said, "The People are so sneaky and scheming; they will find it and use it for their own bad purposes." The others agreed.

Then, the Second Spirit said, "I know, I know where to leave our Powers. Let us leave them at the bottom of the deepest ocean."

"No," the others said, "The People are so sneaky and scheming; they will find it and use it for their own bad purposes." The others agreed.

Finally, the Third Spirit said, "I know, I know where to leave our powers. Let us leave them where they will never think to look for them—let us leave them deep inside themselves."

And that is where they left them, where man would never think to look for them, right below their own noses!

And that is why all humans are blessed with unlimited potential, an ability to dream, and an abundance of love and self-esteem, if they can SEE."

**...From Alita's Journey to Truth—The Younger Years—
The first book in this series by Harry Derbitsky**

- Quotes are from *The Missing Link* written by *Sydney Banks*[1]

*"The wise medicine men in the
Native North American culture
spoke of the world as one spirit,
referring to the creator of all things
as the "Great Spirit"*

*This was their way of explaining
the oneness of life."*

Red Elk reflected for a few moments on this statement.
Then he read the next passage:

*"Thought is a divine tool
that is the link between
you and your divine inheritance
And is at the core
of all your psychological understanding."*

Red Elk tilted his head slightly and asked Alita about this last
passage. Alita said she had found these words to be true.

...From "My Heart Soars" by Chief Dan George, Coast Salish

*Young people
are the pioneers
of new ways.
Since they face
too many temptations
it will not be easy
to know what is best.*

*Of all the teachings we receive
this one is the most important:*

*Nothing belongs to you
of what there is,*

*of what you take,
you must share*

When the winds blow, cottonwood leaves rustle in a way that sounds beautiful. Black Elk used the cottonwood tree many times, when talking about his people.

"I saw that the sacred circle of my people was one of many circles, that all together made one circle...and in the center grew one mighty flowering tree to shelter all the children of one mother and father. I saw that it was holy.

It is a very tall tree with rustling leaves, and the animals and people mingled like relatives. It was filled with singing birds. I heard the wind blowing gently through the tree and singing there. The Sacred Pipe came on eagle wings from the east and stopped beneath the tree, spreading Peace around it."

...www.bluecloud.org/ sacredtree.html

"I like your words and the fact that you have written about your experiences in the lodge.

Our world view or the view of Natives is a holistic one, we see life in all living things—trees, water, everything.

When we are in ceremony (Sweat Lodge), the true purpose is to obtain direction as to how to live on this earth."

...John Delorme, (Black Thunderbird) Sweat Lodge Leader, Aboriginal Education in British Columbia

Alita's Sacred Journey

In the Beginning

Alita was raised by her tender and affectionate Native mother in a small Coast Salish Indian village in British Columbia, Canada. The village, while a fun filled community for a youth, was plagued with the normal social problems of any Native community—alcoholism, drugs, poverty, prejudice, violence, greed, sexual abuse, gossip and personal suffering. Her non-Native father lived in Winnipeg; Alita loved him as he was fun loving and easy going.

Her grandmother, wise Elders and two Shaman or Medicine Men had taught her some of the Old Ways. She had drummed at many PowWow's, including several winter seasons of Si O Win (Coast Salish Longhouse Spirit Dancing), sweated in numerous communities, as well as having been, on occasion, a sweat lodge leader in one Native community. A few years ago, she had become a carrier of the sacred pipe—hers being a particular honor because a wise incarcerated Lakota from a Nevada Prison had sent her his sacred buffalo pipe as a tribute for all her help and guidance. He wrote "*I am truly grateful you accepted the pipe into your heart and life, and yes Alita, the pipe will truly guide you in some very profound experiences providing you remain open. I have found in prison that at times remaining open becomes very difficult because an awakened pipe's purpose is to guide us to the suffering so that we may bring peace in those lives. There is a lot of suffering in prison, out there I imagine there is as well. So use this sacred tool as your guide and with your already deep wisdom you will surely be able to alleviate much suffering."*

As stated, she had come to learn some of the Old Ways, but did not consider herself to be a medicine woman. When asked she simply said she was not one, but she knew a bit about the medicine and healing; as well as possessing some understanding about the sacred nature of the Great Spirit. Many of her friends considered her to be a Dreamer—as she appeared to be able to see into the future.

Her journey had begun at a very early age as she wished to understand how to alleviate some of the suffering of her aunties and uncles. Her own mother's journey had motivated her, even though it was a sad story. Her dear mother had been one of the great ladies of the village, a natural leader with a generous heart, a smile that spread widely across her face, eyes that twinkled when she was happy and filled with a confidence to help and lead people. However, as the years wore on she became stubborn, believing she was always in the right. The ego power of seriousness and weakness had dragged her back into her old nemesis—alcohol. The alcohol had consumed her, and each time Alita saw her, she resembled her mother less and more a drunken Indian living off the dark streets of Vancouver. Remembering the wise teachings and dream of Grandma Ta'7A (pronounced Ta'Ah) when she was a young girl, Alita waited patiently for that future moment when her Mother would extend her mind and heart for help.

Alita had been blessed with exceptionally wise Native and Non-Native teachers in the worlds of Spirit and Mind. She generalized many of her People were spiritually astute, but psychologically unwise. If the People persisted in thinking ugly, insecure thoughts about their relatives, community members and sad past, their psychological lives would not improve, even if their material life did.

She often was heard saying these words:

"Allow your Thoughts to Soar As High as the Eagle Spirit Turning your Dreams into Reality"

Now in her mid 50's, Alita believed all of life is spiritual.

Section 1

Three Different Waves

Chapter 1
The Sweat

(Note: Appendix 1 describes a Sweat from 'Alita's Journey to Truth—The Early Years', for those who wish a more comprehensive understanding of the sacred ceremony)

Not far from where she lived, Native and Non-Natives gathered for a weekly Saturday sweat, led by the wise Cree Elder, Black Fox. Alita shared some of her medicines with Black Fox's wife; including aromatic California sage, which had been mailed to her by a woman healer who counseled Natives in U.S.A. prisons.

For this particular sweat, the ten group members were busy preparing different colored cloth to make strings of tobacco prayer ties, which were then tied primarily at the northern top branches of the lodge. One of the sweat lodge members would sit under these tobacco ties to receive a spiritual healing during the sweat. To her surprise, Black Fox asked Alita to sit there.

The first round began with many red-hot glowing lava rocks being carried into the central pit, followed by the smudging or purification by sweetgrass and cedar on the rocks. Black Fox asked all to say a prayer to assist Alita in her spiritual healing.

Grey Wolf, a Coast Salish Elder, raised both his hands above his head and talked about *Siem*, which means the *Creator of all Spirit*. He mentioned sometimes the word is also used to indicate a Native who understood the Old Ways, including Creator, culture and their interconnection. It could be a carver, or a storyteller or anyone who shows the power and wisdom of the Native culture. "*O Siem* is *Thank You Creator*, and that is something nice to say."

As the first round began, Alita became surprisingly uncomfortable. Normally, a sweat was painless and relaxing for her. The heat seemed to be more intense than usual; Alita was relieved after the first round when the door was opened, and she could feel the cool outside air. The second round was the female round and Alita felt especially queasy and unsettled. This uncomfortable feeling continued throughout the four rounds, with a noticeable relief near the end of the sweat. The drumming in each round had been enjoyable, but her mind was not clear.

Between one of the early rounds, Grey Wolf had mentioned specifically to Alita that life is not only philosophical but also practical, and she could not help but think she did have a tendency to see life from a philosophical perspective.

Later Alita sat beside Billy Joe, who immediately began describing a direct experience he had had regarding his past and his lack of intimacy with his wife. He said, "It is strange how you can do something your whole life and never see it, even though it is in front of your nose continuously. It was fear of success." Alita mentioned she could use some more of that intimacy; as truthfully, she was feeling alone, not having a mate for many years now.

Finally, when the sweat was over, the group was invited into the house for moose lasagna. Alita was famished. The group around the dinner table talked about the Spirits they had seen while in the sweat. Black Fox mentioned two helping eagle spirits, others talked about light and seeing other animal spirits. Billy Joe mentioned how in the second round, he had seen a spirit leave through the door and Black Fox acknowledged in agreement. This was unusual as most spirits entered the sweat. Alita did not pay too much attention to this aspect of the conversation, except to enjoy the talking while devouring the delicious moose lasagna, bannock (fried Indian bread) and apple juice.

Black Fox had asked Alita several times during and after the sweat how she felt. There was no doubt she had been tired and exhausted for much of the sweat. Immediately after the sweat, she had mentioned she felt twenty pounds lighter, however, once at the food table, her exhaustion returned.

As Black Fox was leaving, he whispered directly to Alita, "You know the spirit they were talking about in the second round that flew out the open door of the sweat, well you should sleep well tonight because that spirit came from you—it was something harmful and now you will notice a change."

Alita wondered what it could be!

Chapter 2
Mexico

Alita had been feeling lonely, especially with Christmas fast approaching. Now, she was flying on an airplane from Vancouver, Canada to Cancún, Mexico. Enthusiastically, her sister had extended an invitation to join her for a one-week stay over the Christmas holidays. The free accommodation and a last minute cheap flight for twenty percent of the regular price had clinched the deal.

She would arrive with no preliminary investigation into Cancún, as she did not want any preconceived ideas about this unknown world; she had entered her first sweat lodge with this same attitude. However once on the plane, she could not resist the allure of picking up and reading an attractive travel brochure. She read that Cancún (pronounced can-koon) is a coastal city in Mexico's easternmost state, Quintana Roo. It is a world renowned tourist resort with modern beachfront hotels surrounded by the Bahía de Mujeres (Bay of Women), the Caribbean Sea, and the Nichupte and Bojorquez lagoons.

In the early 1950s, Cancún was a small island just off the Caribbean Sea coast of the Yucatán peninsula, home to three caretakers of a coconut plantation and small Pre-Columbian ruins of the Maya civilization. Development of Cancún started in 1970, and was established as a city in 1972. The city has grown rapidly over the past thirty years to become a city of approximately 600,000 residents, covering the former island and the nearby mainland. Most 'cancunenses' here are from Yucatán and other Mexican states.

She made a mental note that the region's famous Mayan sights are particularly impressive at Uxmal and Chichén Itzá, near the Yucatán state capital of Mérida.

As Alita looked out of the airplane window near the end of the five and half-hour flight, she noticed Cancún was originally jungle, nestled next to the Caribbean Sea. The landing brought a smile to Alita's face, especially when she felt the tropical air. She squeezed her shoulders with delight, as she wrapped her arms around her upper midsection and exclaimed to herself, "Tropical weather in December—perfect!"

Surprisingly, Mexican customs were uncomplicated. However, once in the airport, the scene that greeted her was wildly confusing with tourists negotiating or asking Mexicans a multitude of questions. Her sister had told her there was a bus for $7.50 in American currency (the only American money she foolishly had) which would take her from the airport to the Solymar Beach Resort where she would be staying. This proved to be incorrect, as the actual cost was $9US. Finally after many amusing attempts, she was correctly pointed to a smiling Mexican man and several ladies, where she calmly negotiated her ride for $10 Canadian and $2.50 American. She smiled to herself as these dark faced Mexicans had no difficulty coming to an agreement and seemed to enjoy this style of negotiation. The bus turned out to be one of a series of eight seated vans, which take the thousand's of touristos to their individual hotels on a twelve-mile strip.

31

Alita assessed the Mexicans liked a relaxed touristo who treated them as equals. However, it was obvious they like to 'wheel and deal', thus, she would have to keep her wits about her if she intended to not be fooled out of her pesos. She laughed to herself and said, "I guess it is just part of the fun of being in Mexico". Besides her own People, while different in their approach, were equally scheming and hungry for money.

In about fifteen minutes, the van pulled up to her hotel. The Solymar Beach Resort was the first stop along the immense hotel strip for the eight touristos from Texas, Michigan, Minneapolis, and herself. The driver mentioned, "Located at the southern tip of the hotel zone, the Solymar Beach Resort offers easy access by bus or taxi to downtown Cancún and is at the top of a wide sloping beach leading to the turquoise waters of the open Caribbean. There is a golf course nearby and some interesting local Mayan ruins within walking distance on the edge of the lagoon." To Alita, it looked impressive with its guarded gate to pass through, the adobe wall surrounding the front of the hotel and many palm trees embracing the hotel entrance.

She stepped out of the van, explaining to the driver all she had was a five-dollar American bill, and she was willing to give him a one-dollar tip. He smiled, talked a bit, taking a sizeable wad of American dollars out of his pocket and gave Alita three of them, stopping and looking up into her eyes and saying how about a two-dollar tip to which Alita laughed at and said, "no way" and received her final dollar change. The driver laughingly jumped into his van and drove away to the next hotel on the strip.

Luckily, her sister was standing at the resort's entrance while her husband was sitting several meters away. They hugged and a young Mexican concierge took her two small bags up to room 2209. After one more tip, she was inside a charming and tastefully decorated room with an awe-inspiring view. Being an adventurer, within two days Alita's sister's husband would leave them and head to the Guatemalan jungles.

Her sister casually mentioned the resort was rated 3 ½ to 5 stars by various magazines, but in her opinion it was only, at the highest, a 4 star hotel. Alita was secretly pleased it was not one of those highly priced monster 5 star American hotels with a pretentious atmosphere, with limited vegetation and grounds to walk around in. In her opinion, these pretentious hotels emphasized their size rather than a cozy room, nice surroundings and genuine hospitality, and where she would have to act professionally rather than just 'hanging out'.

Alita was a chameleon. She was financially limited, even though her resumé was notably impressive, having successfully consulted and helped many prosperous non-Native businessmen, government and powerful Native organizations and communities. Alita's treasure was she was equally comfortable with people from all walks of life—rich or poor, Native and non-Native, as she understood the wealthiest riches of life lay profoundly inside every human being. This inner core was alive and healthy in her, and was awakened more and more each day. She was at peace with her finances and content with the understanding the future was still to be written. For some mysterious reason almost all who met Alita thought she was retired and independently wealthy, perhaps associating a relaxed mind and lack of stress with financial prosperity and a retired lifestyle.

Alita was content with the fact that, although her funds were limited, she had sufficient money to enjoy her one week vacation in Cancún and completely washed away any thought except that of an immersion into the holiday feeling of the tropical abundance and exotic nature of Mexico.

As Alita sat out on their second floor lanai outside their room, she was transfixed by the beauty that lay before her. She saw fifty or so palm treetops waving and swaying in the strong tradewinds of the Caribbean, much like a hula dancer would softly and smoothly shift her hips. Just beyond the treetops were two outdoor pools, where guests of the hotel were lying around absorbing the rays of the hot tropical sun. In the middle of the grounds sat a sliding windowed restaurant. Just beyond all of this, was the raging bright turquoise Caribbean Sea with its four to six foot waves making a continual thunderous sound that was soothing and pleasing to Alita's ears, as they crashed onto the shoreline of the talcum powdered white beach. The sky was presently clear of clouds but she later noticed they often blew in and just as quickly back out again by the strong warm winds.

Alita felt a swim and some sun rays by the pool would be a fine introduction to her first day. After unpacking and changing, she descended to the pool area. She laid her beach towel on a lounge chair near the pool and dove athletically into the cool water. It was a bit cold, but invigorating and refreshing. She came out with a smile on her face, and as luck would have it, she sat next to a French Canadian. He mentioned Alita reminded him of his Grandfather with the way she gracefully dived into the pool, hinting his own expanded midriff was now making certain athletic movements more difficult. As they chatted, Alita learned Robert had worked six years with the Inuit as a teacher in Northern Quebec. He added how everyone had told him about the prejudice of the Inuit and yet, he had experienced none of it. The People naturally felt comfortable with him, especially the Elders who loved to tell him stories of the Old Ways.

Robert told Alita a personal story of how he had become divorced and sad, and then experienced a change of mind. He grew content and satisfied that not only was he single, but he would probably remain so for the rest of his life. He grew to understand life was precious, and one day, as if by magic, he was sent north to replace a teacher, a youngish Mexican Canadian woman. They spent four days together supposedly for training, and fell madly in love. They married, now had a seven month son and his happiness has continued to grow—all from the miracle of becoming content inside himself.

Later that day, Alita met his smiling Mexican wife and child, and learned from her almost all Mexicans originate from Aboriginals, although some are Spanish. She informed Alita she was 1/16 Indian, having learned some of these traditions from her grandmother. However, she did add that, in most cases, the rich Mexicans were light skinned while those of dark skin were often poor, and that her own family was relatively wealthy.

Upon saying goodbye to Robert and his wife who were staying at their father's condominium in the resort, Alita went upstairs and began a pleasant conversation with her sister. She mentioned what Robert had said about the Great Spirit having a special gift for his psyche.

Her sister responded, "Please define psyche."

Alita paused and thought for a moment, looking into the distant sky. She gathered herself and stated, "To me, psyche is a psychological way of describing soul. Soul is pure Spirit, and exists before any cultural psyche."

Her sister asked, "Please explain the relationship between culture and psyche."

Alita responded, "In my philosophy of life, all babies are born pure and innocent. Then from the 1st second past birth, they begin learning their culture. Culture is simply a series of commonly agreed upon thoughts and values expressing themselves within a form we call culture. Really, culture is a common understanding by a group of people. For instance, the

Germans learn to be hard working, the Danish learn to be tolerant and the Americans learn to be patriotic. We could say there is an Indian psyche, which intuitively understands the ceremony of the Oneness of life, how each rock, frog and tree is Spirit and how the Great Spirit creates all. The Jewish psyche understands the feeling of family, of one people, and a common connectiveness to community throughout the globe. These different expressions of cultural values are respected and honored by their followers, yet they all point to the same truth.

Inside every human being, before culture and any other form, is the highest consciousness, that which we call Soul and it connects us to the Oneness of Life, and of course, my dear sister, if there is Oneness, there cannot be separation. So all cultures are individual expressions of this Oneness, and it is only man who believes differently and expresses prejudice."

Her sister nodded with an interesting look on her face, and decided it was time to make some coffee.

As her sister began to relax over the following days, her nervous habits of 'busy thinking' slowed down. She began to lie in the sun, exercise every day in the pool with the Mexican guide and other touristos, and generally experience waves of happiness. Alita gave her a book on wisdom; she peacefully read it.

Chapter 3
Waves 1 and 2

Wave 1—Caribbean Waves

Later, Alita took a walk and stood at the top center of the patio of the resort, holding onto the fence, which overlooked the sensual Caribbean Sea. It was an exciting site. Palm trees were in front of her, creating a peaceful sway in the warm tradewinds. Yet not more than twenty-five feet away, a beach of the purest, cleanest white sand stood, and just a little farther on, the thunderous waves of the Caribbean were raging onto the shore. The waves were a clean, clear turquoise hue topped with numerous frothy whitecaps. Tanned touristos were standing near or playing in the impressive and eye-popping waves. Before, she had noticed a Red Flag sticking out of the sand and asked the lifeguard the significance of this. Alita learned the flags indicated the level of danger from the waves, with White being the gentlest, Black being the most perilous, and the existing Red, second most dangerous.

Alita, just a few hours ago, had poured her joyful spirit into those waves, laughing and expressing great smiles of rapture. She went up to waist high, on solid sand with wave after wonderful wave pouring over her body.

Then it happened! An unexpected titanic wave came. The overpowering undertow carried her ten feet out to sea over her head. Now, the mighty six-foot waves continuously poured onto her head and accosted her body. She swam with all her might but could not move forward as the force of the waves returning out to sea made it impossible for her to move. Now she *knew* she was close to drowning. She yelled and screamed, desperately seeking help from the watchers on shore. The beach was not very far away, yet too far away to swim to. The waves seemed a million times stronger than her, pouring over her head every few seconds, huge waves of thunderous power. She was exhausted.

Then she saw a lifeguard enter the water! The waves were so powerful that he could only travel towards her a few inches at a time, but she had hope now! The waves continued to pound onto her head and she felt as if she was being pushed to the bottom of the sea.

Alita intuitively relaxed.

Suddenly, she experienced a *'moment of inspiration'*—a calm, relaxed mind would expend the least amount of her limited energy and give her the greatest chance to come out of this experience alive. Immediately, she thought of catching the top of a mighty wave and riding it closer to the beach. She calmly attempted to ride the waves, convinced this was her greatest chance of surviving. Six or seven times she failed! "Where is that lifeguard," she wondered? She was now swallowing so much salt water and her energy was nearly depleted. She glanced and saw that the lifeguard continued to inch forward, held back by the crushing power of the incoming waves. Then, because *her mind was distracted*, a giant wave accidentally caught and carried her five to ten feet closer to shore and her large toe *only just* touched solid sand and ground which was just enough to allow her to barely rest for a couple of seconds. She was exhausted and the waves continued to crash over her but not nearly as rapidly as before, then she was pulled farther out to sea. Finally, the lifeguard was beside her! She thankfully put her hand on his shoulder for support, as her energy was totally depleted. Then, holding onto him, he pulled her to shore where she lay spent; she rested and regained her strength.

She was breathing heavily but felt strangely exhilarated, almost like she thought riding on the world's largest roller coaster would be. She was energized by the life the sea gave, but did not underestimate who was in charge. "The sea is simply too strong an adversary for weak individual humans," she thought. "The Spirit of the individual human is strong, but without the Great Spirit's help, she would have been dead."

"Being alive felt wonderful," she thought as she trekked back to their apartment.

She was tired and exhausted, encrusted with sand, but with an incredible tale to tell. When she told her sister and her sister's husband the story, they could not quite believe it, and expressed a true look of horror in their eyes. They had thought when Alita had walked into their room with eyes full of fire and vigor that something wonderful had happened.

Alita actually was a bit surprised at their alarmed reaction to her story.

However, this near death experience had been surrealistic to her; an illusionary dream that appeared not to have happened, but like all dreams, had undeniable Spirit Power associated with it.

She liked this Mexico; it was alive with the Spirit of the People. The Mexicans seemed obsessed with money. Yet they looked and had the exotic feeling that Aborigine's have, loved the sun, and enjoyed saying 'hola' (hello) to her.

Wave 2—Sickness

The next morning Alita woke up feeling surprisingly tired. The exhaustion of her near death experience in the sea seemed to have beaten her down physically. Her natural resistance against illness had been dramatically compromised and she also knew she had swallowed too much salt water.

Her sister had arranged for the two of them to go on a tour of the famous Mayan ruins and pyramids, Chichén Itzá (pronounced chee-chehn eet-sah). Alita was looking forward to the mystical stories about the Mexican Indians and seeing the ancient sites. The tour bus picked them up at 7:30 a.m., but instead of taking them directly to the ruins, detoured to a marketplace in downtown Cancún where many typical Mexican items were sold. There, they looked around at the many colorful booths, while waiting for their new bus to leave. After a several hour bus ride, they arrived in a small town at another vendor's market where more Mexican trinkets were sold and where she purchased a Mayan war chant CD. Then they were back on the bus, finally arriving at noon just outside of Chichén Itzá at a local hotel. A scrumptious homemade Mexican lunch and entertainment by a local band singing traditional Mexican songs pleased the visitors. Subsequently, they did not arrive at the ruins until 1:30 and, by that time; Alita had become totally exhausted and nauseous.

As she walked, she almost collapsed, barely able to hear the Mexican guide tell the thirty tourists how this immense pyramid was 91 steps high, in the four directions (91 x 4) = 364 and 1 square on the top making up the calendar year of 365 days. The entrance was facing east just as sweat lodges generally are. The exact angles of the pyramid were identical to those in Egypt. She also found her clapping of hands had produced an echoing sound as she faced these ancient ruins. "These Mayan Indians were obviously sophisticated scientists in their knowledge of astrology, astronomy and the Universe," thought Alita.

The guide continued, "This archaeological site is rated among the most important of the Maya culture and covers an area of approximately six square miles where hundreds of buildings once stood. Originating in the Yucatan around 2600 BC, the Mayans rose to prominence around 250 AD in present-day southern Mexico, Guatemala, northern Belize and western Honduras. The Maya evolved the only true writing system native to the Americas and were masters of mathematics; they were noted as well for elaborate and highly decorated ceremonial architecture, including temple-pyramids, palaces and observatories, all built without metal tools, beasts of burden or the wheel. Building on the inherited inventions and ideas of earlier civilizations, the Maya developed astronomy, calendrical systems and hieroglyphic writing. They were skilled farmers, clearing large sections of tropical rain forest and, where groundwater was scarce, building sizable underground reservoirs for the storage of rainwater. The Maya were equally skilled as weavers and potters, and cleared routes through jungles and swamps to foster extensive trade networks with distant peoples."

There were many other amazing scientific facts but Alita had become too sick to hear. She collapsed onto nearby grass and fell asleep, wondering if the spirits were forbidding her to listen to these ancient stories. When she awoke, her group had disappeared and was no longer in sight. She groggily walked back to where the bus was waiting to return them to Cancún. Her sister had also returned and had a huge smile on her face; she had climbed the pyramids which was no small feat considering how scary the steps were to climb down, as they appeared to face straight down when you descended them. Her sister had explored these sights with glee and pleasure.

The following few days Alita grew sicker and sicker having waves of fever, sore grating throat and vomiting. Alita realized she was faced with an *interesting choice*. She could stay in bed and be sick, or she could continue to enjoy her holiday. Since this holiday was too precious to waste, she was determined not to forego her holiday feeling. She accepted her waves of sickness as they came, accommodating her high fever, furry throat, a heavy head and limited energy. She relaxed and continued to rest as needed. She found deep within the recesses of her soul, a peace and discipline that provided the only answer she needed, i.e. an ability to truly enjoy her holiday despite her limitations. She entered an 'altered state of consciousness' where, when the overpowering waves of the sickness arrived, just like the omnipotent Caribbean waves had, she totally relaxed, enduring the sickness. This gentle approach allowed the numerous waves of sickness to flow through her as quickly as possible. Sometimes they would linger for an hour, and then she would rest or sleep, and at other times they would quickly move along out of her body and she was able to go for a swim or enjoy the day. At night her body's energy level lowered; she often found herself with a strong fever and violent hoarse cough, and then, upon retiring to bed, relaxation overpowered the sickness and she slept soundly.

Suddenly, the most amazing transformation began to occur. The greater her sickness, the more intimate she and her sister became. They would begin the day with delicious Mexican fruits like strawberry papaya, mango and pineapple with coffee for breakfast, while they chatted. Her sister loved to talk, and now that Alita was so 'bagged', she relaxed and simply listened to her sister's points of view. She grew to appreciate and respect her sister's friendship. Each day her sister became happier and more cheerful, years seemed to drop off her weary and tired face. Her sister was now relaxing, and not trying to figure out how to maximize her holiday with one adventure after another.

Alita thought to herself, "Could it be that in the past, I had too many opinions and an overactive mind, which blocked the quiet feelings of the Spirit to work its magic between the two of us?" It seemed her sister loved a quieter Alita.

Alita was learning something very simple and meaningful. If she relaxed with the waves of discomfort and sickness, she would experience an altered state of consciousness, which protected her. This would allow her to totally enjoy her experience (because she was simply looking out at her sickness, with her mind in neutral and relatively no thought). Even though, normally this sickness would have made it impossible for her to enjoy herself, she had uncovered the 'eye of the hurricane'.

When she returned home she would tell her friends she had totally enjoyed Mexico, even though she almost died in the waves and became very sick halfway through the trip. Her friends would be amazed at her horrendous holiday happenings; laugh at her because they saw a sparkle in her eyes and youthful enthusiasm in her demeanor.

Chapter 4
Work

"Choose a job you love and you will never have to work a day in your life"… Confucius

During one of her peaceful days, she walked down to the pool to relax. Robert was also at the poolside. He ended up laughing at her drowning story and then graciously invited Alita to his Mexican wife's parent's home near the Yucatán capital city of Mérida for dinner, to which she graciously accepted. She was excited and pleased with this invitation. She loved experiencing other cultures, and meeting Robert's family was truly a gem she would always cherish.

A few hours later, Robert and his family arrived by car and picked up Alita at the front door of the resort. Robert began chatting and mentioned they where going to a hacienda[4], to which Alita asked, "Doesn't that mean house in Mexican?"

Robert told her it also had other meanings. Now, as the car rolled out of Cancún and over a several hour drive, Robert began to describe aspects of old Mexico. "It is in Mexico that the hacienda system can be considered to have its origin in 1529, when the Spanish crown granted to Hernán Cortés the title of

Marquis of the Valley of Oaxaca, which entailed a tract of land that included all of the present state of Morelos. Significantly to you Alita, the grant included all the Indians then living on the land and power of life and death over every soul on his domains.

The owner of a hacienda was called the hacendado or patrón. Aside from the small circle at the top of the hacienda society, the remainder was peones (serfs), campesinos (peasants), or mounted ranch hands variously called vaqueros or gauchos. The peones worked land that belonged to the patrón, whereby the campesinos worked small holdings, and owed a portion of its harvest to the patrón.

Haciendas were abolished by law in 1917 during the Mexican revolution, but remnants of the system still affect Mexico today. In rural areas, the wealthiest people typically live the style of the old patrón even though their wealth these days derives more from capitalistic enterprises."

He concluded by saying, "In Mérida there are generally two classes of Mexicans—rich and poor," and then yelled out to Alita, "Here is Papa's little home!!"

The elderly father, Pedro, was an extremely wealthy Mexican, who had experienced much personal sickness. After the customary introductions, Robert's family and Alita were escorted into a majestic living room. Glancing around the spacious living room, Alita noted that like the hacienda walls outside, these living-room walls were gessoed a dazzling alabaster. The only adornments on the walls were two small crucifixes and a large rectangular mirror in an elaborately carved teak frame. Scattered around the spacious room were four octagonal tables of matching teak, each surrounded by a trio of straight-back armchairs upholstered to soft jet-black leather. A matching leather couch faced a long low narrow table also of teak. Against each of three walls stood an ebony chest feathering a dozen smaller drawers with brass handles. The fourth wall opened into a vast dining hall at the centre of which was a spectacularly long mahogany table and matching straight back armchairs upholstered with leather seats and backs. A filled crystal brandy decanter, surrounded by eight crystal goblets, stood in the middle of a round silver serving tray in the center of the long narrow teak table.

Several sitting Mexican guests were introduced to the arriving guests, and an engaging conversation began. Alita joined into this light-hearted conversation until the subject of work and the lower class was mentioned. Pedro became rather stiff, stating he had no time or patience for the lazy, lower-class peasants who did not want to work. He felt work was the solution to everything, just as many upper-class Mexicans, Americans and Canadians do.

"Put them to work and that will solve all their problems," Pedro resolutely concluded.

As Alita vehemently disagreed with Pedro, she diplomatically walked away from the conversation. She understood that debate on this subject would result in an uncomfortable feeling, which might easily erupt into an argument. She did not want to offend the hospitality of this lovely family and their friends.

Upon her returning a few minutes later, Pedro turned to Alita saying he would value her opinion on the topic. She hesitated, softly saying, "We are on opposite sides on this subject and I do not wish to insult you in your own home. I know I will not change my mind, and I really do not believe you want to change yours, so let us agree to disagree and continue with the fine feelings of the evening the Creator has so graciously given to us."

But Pedro insisted, saying, "There should not be any problem if we debate from an investigative point of view."

So, reluctantly, Alita stated her People were often classified as lazy and lacking the will to work, yet her own personal experience was exactly the opposite. Her People were extremely hard working when they felt appreciated or had a reason to work. She felt, for them, success had more to do with their psychological makeup or self-esteem. All humans are prisoners of their own thoughts, yet if seen wisely; it (thought) is the master key to happiness.

Pedro was puzzled.

"Let me try to explain these statements with an extreme example," Alita countered.

"My sister and I were walking in Cancún the other day and we saw a sad sight. A young Mexican man sat in anguish; his head drooped down, his hands and fingers moving feverishly through his hair, over and over again as in an insane stupor. When we returned fifteen minutes later, this man was still sitting in the same spot trying to drive crazy inner voices from his mind, even clenching his fist and banging his head with his fist. It looked like he was attempting to chase away millions of mosquitoes and flies, but of course it was simply mental thoughts that were causing him this suffering. If he actually realized or experienced this, he would have been instantly cured or healed.

Pedro, would you say this man could succeed in a job interview? Was this man 'psychologically ready' to work, or was he a prisoner of his own thoughts?"

Pedro shook his head, unsure of the answer.

Alita continued, "This is how many unemployed and poor People are, except not as extreme as this sad soul. The Natives are very spiritual People, possessing an elevated understanding of how the Great Spirit created us and gave us the gift of life and a free will to think whatever we want. However, when my People's negative or impure thinking interferes with their natural spiritual essence or psyche, then they experience stress, unhealthy feelings, and even mental disease. Their 'will to work' is weakened, not from laziness but from a weakened spirit. Low self-esteem or a self-esteem crisis can be the result.

When I taught a Self-Esteem and Employment Program to my People, it became obvious their thinking had more to do with not working than their lack of experience. While they all wanted jobs desperately, almost all had serious doubts about their ability to work, false beliefs about their own capabilities, and in many cases, disenabling thoughts from their past. These factors, combined with the fact that much of their personal life was imperfect, seemed to create a false image in their minds that attaining successful work was nearly impossible. Yet, I could see how incredibly talented and capable they were. My job was to get them to see their own health and talent inside themselves.

Without a feeling of confidence and pride no one can hope to touch their unlimited potential. Could any successful businessman, including you, succeed without this feeling, Pedro? Without this understanding about self-esteem, solutions most often revolve around punishing people or forcing them to do what they do not want to do or are not ready to do. When the poor people of Mexico awaken to their Spiritual Identity, then the greatest natural resource of Mexico will be released. Once the poor people believe in themselves, they will be able to change Mexico's destiny, ensuring a place for all hard-working and creative Mexicans.

That is how I see it, Pedro. Employment programs in our communities benefit those who are mentally ready to work. Many others are in transition, either from anger and disgust about past bad habits, or from immaturity. They are not ready to work in our cruel, and oftentimes, cold world. The Native ways teach when the four directions of our inner wheel move in harmony with the

Universe, our spiritual, mental, physical, and intellectual balance are restored. Material gain and work are not always enough. However, Pedro, I do absolutely agree that work has a lot to do with happiness, and perhaps this is your viewpoint."

Pedro nodded and felt it was time to enjoy the snacks and coffee that were set out nearby. A few minutes later, Pedro turned suddenly to Alita saying, "But doesn't work keep our minds active and alive, and isn't that healthy?"

"Yes, of course," said Alita. "Our minds need productive activity just like flowers need water. However, there can be other factors as well, and I will tell you a true story to demonstrate this.

There was a time when a very wise non-Native could not get a job in Canada for over a year. He received welfare from the government, he often dug ditches, and performed other menial labor jobs once or twice a week to supplement his meager income. He grew quite cynical of his life since his friends and his personal thoughts painted him to be a loser. After all, he had no car, no money, no job, no girlfriend, only one or two friends, lots of debt, and one dear son whom he loved and who loved him greatly.

However, he was growing tired of always being sad, and one day, as he sat in his living room, his inner voice spoke to him, telling him he'd had enough of this 'stupid seriousness' of trying to become a success. He instantly became content with every aspect of his life, recognizing his life was all right and may never change. He became his own best friend, enjoying the quietness of his continuous idle moments. His own thoughts delighted him. When his treasured son and his friends came to his apartment, he cheerfully gave smiles, pop, food, and happiness to the 16-year-old boys who seemed to gravitate there. Even though he was broke and unemployed, he was content.

Shortly thereafter, he received a telephone call for a job interview as an Executive Director for an Aboriginal organization. For five days he mentally prepared since he did not want to arrive at the interview worried or insecure. He mentally went over what technical questions he might be asked. He became totally confident and secure, even though he could not afford to have his suit dry cleaned. The interview was a powerful success, as it came and went.

The next day, while he was digging sand for just $50 dollars a day because he needed food money, a thought surfaced into his consciousness. He realized this digging job was a total waste of time for a man of his talent and intellect. He went home that day knowing he would never work at that type of job again. Later that evening, he received the news he had been waiting for, and the next day he started his job as an Executive Director.

Our Elders teach us, "Do what you want to do and do it now—don't wait for tomorrow because sometimes tomorrow doesn't come."

So the answer lies not with what a person is doing, but what state of mind he is doing it in. Yes, work is great, but if you are lucky enough to see inside yourself, you will naturally seek not only work, but also satisfactory work with the creativity, teamwork, and communication activities that are required to satisfy your soul. After all, people are like flowers. They want to bloom, and also they want to dream.

Now, Pedro, would a person succeed as a businessman with a bad attitude or not being psychologically comfortable with himself? I am sure you can see a feeling of hopelessness would produce a person that appears lazy and misdirected. Yet, when the pessimism changes to optimism, there is no lack of energy, creativity, and passion for work or success. Thus, the human journey is psychological, but I would call it a spiritual psychological journey rather than assigning the concepts of present-day psychology. In my opinion, the latter is an antiquated system of studying past behaviours and labeling people as being permanently sick.

As wise medicine men teach us, at the centre of our Sacred Wheel is our free will to think whatever we want. When we go in the wrong direction with our thoughts, we, as human beings, get out of harmony with the Great Spirit. This is where we have all those mental problems, because we get out of touch with the 'balance of life.' An insecure and troubled mind is the result."

As the visit was drawing to a close, Alita looked profoundly into Pedro's eyes and said how much she had enjoyed their time together.

Just before leaving, Pedro said to Robert, "Alita is a very special woman. Thank you for bringing her today. We all feel her coming here brings honor to this house."

Very early the next morning upon arising, she reflected on yesterday's stimulating visit, as she looked out of her second floor balcony window. Today, the winds were blowing, the trees swaying, the ocean was creating stereo sounds of waves crashing on the sandy beaches, the clouds were intermittent, and the ocean had turned a darkish blue and seemed to go on forever; these were the sights and sounds of this early Christmas morning. The restaurant in the middle of this oasis had just turned on its lights indicating the activities of the day were slowly getting under way, as it was 6 a.m. The palm-tree trunks were covered in bright white Christmas lights creating a surrealistic effect against this oncoming Christmas day that promised to be hot and windy.

Alita wondered what Mexicans did on Christmas day. After lunch, she began walking down the twelve-mile powdery sandy beach and came to the public beach, which was not controlled by the hotels. It was filled with Mexican families who had come after lunch to enjoy the rays of the sun. The ocean was filled with Mexican children and teenagers laughing, wrestling and throwing the fine talcum powdered sand at each other, which stuck to their hot and wet bodies and faces. They dove into the warm water bouncing up with great white toothy smiles on their dark faces. Joy and happiness was everywhere, and for the first time since arriving in Cancún, Alita felt like it was Christmas!

Later that day, Alita and her sister telephoned their father in Winnipeg, Manitoba. As usual, he was chipper, full of energy, and pleased that Alita had made it to Cancún and was enjoying herself. They wished him a happy birthday as he turned eighty on this day of Christmas. It was one of the family's stories that came out now and again to tease him—his birthday being on Christmas Day and him being Jewish. Alita and her sister were both glad they were able to talk to him that day and he seemed extremely pleased to hear from both of them.

Chapter 5

Wave 3—Death

On returning home, Alita was blessed with compelling memories of her trip to Mexico. After several days of being seriously ill, she started to recover much of her health, but not all, for the sickness lingered on for another several weeks.

She described Mexico as a land of contrasts and unpredictability. In truth, Mexico is a paradise with near perfect weather, idyllic water and scenery; however, the combination of different food, water and air, plus her near death experience, had brought sickness to her. The Mexican People are exotic and fun loving. Yet one had better watch their wallet for they are masters at conniving you out of a few American dollars or pesos. They loved playing the game of business, yet their country is a contrast of ultra rich and poor, with a petite middle class. Perhaps 20% speak reasonable English, 40% speak limited English and the remainder none at all. They are masters at fooling you, yet you could fool them—it was all part of being in Mexico.

She would finish by saying to her friends if a tourist only saw the deceptiveness of the Mexican people; they would miss out on the greatest asset in all of Mexico, the beauty of its People. The People continually offered her advice and assistance, and if Alita had become intent only on not being swindled out of her money, she would not have been open to its many pearls. For example, at the supermarket one day a smiling young man had walked up to her sister and herself, and helped them to choose a quality Mexican coffee from his home province. Another lady instructed them on buying peppers, which would not burn their tongues. Three other girls had kindly helped with their overloaded groceries on the bus, and others had continually flashed warm, rich smiles, which touched their hearts.

Shortly after her return, she received the following e-mail from her sister:

'Can hardly believe it, only 1 week left. Time flies when you are having a good time. Went to Xcaret with 2 ladies. It was amazing. Snorkeled an underground river with caves & fish. Saw the most spectacular night show. It started with a Tribal Indian show with sweetgrass. Very mystical. It continued with singing and dancing from all the Mexican provinces. I loved it. Weather here is the same. Windy, sunny, cloudy & hot. I love it!

You would not believe what happened on the beach yesterday. It was extremely windy with a BLACK flag. I went outside and there was this huge crowd. I looked way down in the ocean and saw a head bobbing. 3 lifeguards went out. The waves were at least 20 feet high. It took our lifeguard about 5 minutes to get to the person. The other lifeguards could not get there. He rescued him but it took about 1 hour, before the young man could move or walk. He was a strong man about 30 years old. Very lucky to have our lifeguard. The others could not do it.'

Alita thought, "That could have been me. I could have died!"

Life moves on and one week after Alita returned from Mexico, the telephone rang late at night. Half asleep, she just listened and heard the news from her sister that their father had died in the middle of the night. Two hours later, she was back on the telephone to her sister making arrangements to fly today on the first available flight to Winnipeg. Talking to her sister and feeling her sister's immense sadness brought tears to Alita's eyes and heart. Now it was starting to strike home. Her father, who she thought would live forever, had gone to the Spirit World.

The airplane arrived to a snowy, windless and cold Winnipeg; however, it was impressive and looked pristine. Snow covered everything, including all the trees and the air was much fresher and drier than Vancouver's. While it was -15 degrees Fahrenheit (which would indicate a negative chill factor), it felt warm. Later, Alita noticed as the temperature dropped further to -31 degrees and it still felt warm. It seemed Winnipeg was only cold when the wind was blowing. During her visit, the days displayed not a whisper of wind. Also, there was a total silence, almost like being in the middle of Northern Indian reservations. On most streets, because almost everyone was inside their homes or in a car driving on the main roads, not a sound could be heard. This warmness and startling silence brought peace to Alita.

She walked over to a magnificent elm tree; the tips of its snowy branches drooping downwards contributing to the overall graceful umbrella-like silhouette. She placed a hand on the mottled ash-gray bark of the elm, sensing the eternal Power of the ancient tree.

Her father's death permeated everywhere. She kept having waves of sadness, but she utilized her understanding to relax. She did not pretend she was not sad when the waves of sadness poured into her being. When she felt like crying, she felt the heaviness death brings to a loved one's heart, and would sit in this feeling and allow the healing power of sadness and tears to cleanse her soul. Then, just like the Mexican sickness, the pain would pass and she would share happiness, peace and contentment with her family. In fact, laughter and enjoyment were being felt as they experienced that a family could enjoy themselves even in times of sadness. She and her sister had drawn close and used each other for support. The trip to Mexico had bonded them together, almost as a preparation for the passing away of their father.

Two days after her arrival, her father's funeral was held. Alita had asked to speak at the funeral, and she prepared for a little while the night before, writing down points she did not want to forget to say about this wonderful man. In her talks and lectures, she almost always talked freely without preparation, but this was too important and she wanted to be comfortable talking in front of her father's friends and relatives.

The next morning, she was sitting with her family in the synagogue as the funeral began. The woman cantor (a chazzan [cantor] is the person who leads the congregation in prayer and song) had an extraordinarily beautiful voice as she began singing in Hebrew and tears poured down Alita's face. This was so final, this was not a movie or someone else—this was her father. The feelings overpowered and suffocated her and she began to doubt her ability to talk. Luckily her half-brother and her sister's best friend were to talk first and Alita, being the oldest, would be the last. The waves of her father's spirit seemed to pour over her and she regained her equilibrium; this was wisdom.

Now the rabbi (a rabbi is a teacher, rather than a priest, sufficiently educated in halakhah [Jewish law] and tradition) asked Alita to come forward; as it was her time to talk. She rose and walked slowly to the pulpit, looking out at the two hundred people who had come. She felt vulnerable, but as was her way, her confidence prevailed.

She began:

"I would like to say a few words about Dad. He would have been so happy to see so many of his friends and relatives here, he loved people and they always lifted his spirits."

She talked about how happy her father was the last time he spoke with her and her sister when they were in Mexico; how he died just like he had wanted by working right to the end of his life; how her Dad had no prejudice in his heart and had taught his children this. She recalled how he loved being Jewish but was equally comfortable with all non-Jewish people. She told an amusing story of how her father loved to play cards and she talked about how her Dad was not a survivor, but a winner.

She concluded by saying, "Dad had a great heart and a great laugh, and now I ask you all to lift your hands with me and look to the sky because Dad's spirit is here right now and say, "Well done Charlie, you did it right, you followed your own heart and brought love and understanding to your family and friends, WELL DONE."

A light feeling seemed to permeate the synagogue. Onlookers appeared relaxed and peaceful. A new wave flowed into Alita, but this time it was peaceful happiness. This talk had helped her, just as it did when she spoke at her best friend's wake sometime ago.

Two Memories of Death

Alita had been privileged to experience two deaths in her life, which eased her through her father's passing away.

The first was her dear grandmother who had gone to the hospital for a routine checkup and never left. Alita had been alone with her in the hospital room, praying to the Great Spirit, when, suddenly, her grandmother had died. She had seen the Spirit leave her grandmother's body—a physical body that instantly became an empty shell. The Spirit was real, like a gaseous form, and *she had seen and experienced it* for perhaps a second or two, as it lifted above the empty body and rose. There was no doubt in her mind the body lying beside her in the hospital bed was not her grandmother any longer. The expressionless face did not look like her any more and Alita knew her grandmother had left for the Spirit World.

The second was of her best friend who had had cancer. He had 90% of his throat and all of his chin removed by surgery; and still lived seven years longer than the doctor's prognostication. In fact, the last year was the happiest of his life and the greatest year of their friendship. Without a doubt, he had learned how to live life stress free, as any large amount of stress guaranteed an earlier death. In his last hospital stay, he confided to Alita saying, "Death is nothing to be afraid of. What happens when we die is we go into the Oneness with the Great Spirit, experience this, and then return to earth as a newborn baby."

Remembering his words, obviously her best friend was still here on earth, except in a new body. 'To be honest, the old one wasn't much good anyway' Alita commented to herself.

Chapter 6
Alita's Reflections on Healing

As Alita reflected on her experiences in Mexico and Winnipeg, she realized true *healing* has two aspects to it:

Firstly, one must find *'a spiritual/positive feeling'* i.e. calmness, relaxation, contentment and happiness, or as the sages say, "go inside and experience your essence". This is the primary experience.

Secondly, once we have rediscovered our spiritual essence, we must grow in our awareness of *'the role and effect of thought'* for the purpose of being able to maintain balance or equilibrium between the Spirit world and our personal world. This second aspect allows us to share the spiritual feeling with ourselves. Healthy thoughts lead to a healthy life—**the Creator's Guarantee**.

Many of her friends, who were trapped by alcoholism, heavy drug addiction or despair, would inevitably experience many spiritual feelings, especially when they temporarily grew tired of their bad habits. However, they quickly walked back into their addiction or away from the healing powers within because they RE-IGNITED the same old patterns of thinking—thus, recreating the same old feelings and old reality they had recently left behind.

Also, many of her friends would experience powerful and undeniable spiritual feelings during spiritual ceremonies, such as the sweat lodge. However, once they walk out of the sweat lodge, many would leave behind those genuine spiritual feelings they had experienced by simply thinking about their old life, its problems and all the past circumstances. If they truly saw how ridiculous this was, they would not take their past so seriously. She was convinced that past stale thoughts lead to or cause sickness. (To Alita, the Past was exactly the same thing as when her grandmother died, and left her body as an empty shell without a spirit. If we leave our negative Past alone and do not think about it, then it becomes lifeless).

Only we can put life into these memories. The true teachers of her People would say, humans have a free will to think whatever they want and when their personal thoughts follow the Black Road instead of the Red Road, they are out of balance with the Sacred Wheel &/or the Great Spirit. That is when stress and bad habits are experienced. When our thoughts are in harmony with the Great Spirit, existence of life as a sacred gift is obvious.

ONE THOUGHT, ONE MIND, ONE BEING—GOD

Section 2

A Man of a Different Flavor

Chapter 7
Divorce

"The way I see it, if you want the rainbow,
you gotta put up with the rain"...Dolly Parton

Alita thought back to seven years prior; she had been married
for twenty-three years, bearing two children, when one day her
husband suddenly demanded a divorce. Truthfully, over time, the
intimacy between them had soured due to constant arguments.

In the early years of the marriage Alita and her husband shared
exquisite feelings. They worked harmoniously together, making
many wise decisions and sharing wonderful experiences of home
life, childbirth and travel. She had come to accept her husband's
intense opinions, for after all, she loved him and saw him as an
excellent father. Also, in her mind, he possessed many other
redeeming qualities such as exceptionally high ethical values, but
was simply too serious minded.

Except for the last few years, the relationship was highlighted
by a lot of fun family times, especially with their children. Alita
mostly chose the road of sharing positivity and accommodating

her husband's stubborn mind—the rewards were substantial. A few years before the divorce, Alita made a very *unwise* decision. She decided the time had come to try and change her partner. She would no longer give into what she perceived as her partner's immovable and inflexible requests. When they disagreed, she, just as he, would strongly voice contrasting opinions and demand equal rights. She was tired of always being the one to say, "I am sorry" or that "he was always right". She decided he must change as well as her; she decided to aggressively assert herself.

This decision did not have anything to do with the fact she was a woman, it could have been reversed. She simply felt she had to project her feelings and needs as strongly as her husband did, and thus, began to establish a pattern of disagreement and fighting.

Many women would later say she was simply establishing her boundaries and independence or that she was better off without him, but she came to understand the foolishness of those statements.

That decision cost the marriage, and from that day forward, the fights and anger between the two grew proportionally stronger, until they were fiercely at odds. Everyone in the house suffered, along with the children.

In truth, Alita suffered the most because she became more and more confused. She established an effective playacting role to her friends, relatives and herself, pretending everything was OK, when it was not. Negative thoughts were constantly raging in her mind. Her confidence was at an all-time low and her own lack of professional success contributed to this low state of self-esteem. She had become a victim or a prisoner of her own negative thinking patterns and this insecurity was fueled by her husband's constant criticisms and complaints. Interestingly, she came to believe if she had remained secure, which was her way and well within her capabilities, she would have diffused much of her husband's negativity and guided him to positive feelings within himself.

Then, just before the final separation, her husband suggested they seek counseling from a trusted psychologist, in order to help Alita adjust to living alone. He felt eventually she would come to realize this divorce would be for the best, not only for him but for her as well. Alita went in the hope of reconciliation and a return to a happy, intimate marriage. It was not to be, as her husband was adamant about a final separation.

However, during this time of counseling many of her personal thoughts quieted down and Alita began to reclaim her own spiritual birthright. She discovered in the confines of her quiet mind two very important points, which were to change her life forever.

Firstly, she saw that even though she was in a psychological state of turmoil, with many, many *ridiculous thoughts*, in between were many *wise thoughts*. Before, when her mind was racing with insecurity and low self-esteem, she could not tell which thoughts were wise and which ones were foolish, as they all felt the same in that wild state of confusion and turmoil. Now, she could. All of sudden, Alita had re-found her rudder to guide herself through the storm. She would consciously use the wise thoughts to guide her home, and discard the unwise ones.

Secondly, Alita had always been keenly interested in helping her Native People alleviate their suffering. She had previously approached the Native world with the idea that a communal approach would be most effective to solving all their social and human problems, since the People are community oriented. Now she saw it differently. Many members in the community were experiencing psychological dysfunctionality just as she was, supported by a harsh and negative past. She saw the solution required a spiritual-mental healing, individual by individual, rather than a group approach. Just as her own experience had taught her, first she must find a healing within herself, and then she could go on to help others.

This second realization created a myriad of employment opportunities for Alita, some of which included going into various Native remote communities, with a renowned and extremely calm psychologist. They provided, from their level of understanding, a healing service. Alita loved working as part of a team, being mentored and gaining experience as she slowly developed into becoming a professional counselor.

She was learning to help her people access their knowledge, rather than lecture on how to become healthy. The psychologist she worked with was wise, but Alita intuitively understood what he taught was not, by itself, profound enough to help her People, for 'mental healing and sacredness' must be connected together for her People to be healed.

Now that the separation with her husband was a fact, Alita began to live alone. She made several key decisions. The first was pivotal to her growth. She was clear about the cause of the divorce; *it was in her thinking.* She knew love was the answer, not fighting. In the marriage all she had had to do was step towards a loving feeling with forgiveness, and the fighting would have gradually stopped. Now, she knew she could have worked wisely with her ex-husband, while accommodating and respecting her own needs.

Later, this explanation was often confusing to her friends, especially regarding their own unhappy relationships. They felt the fault lay with their spouses by at least fifty per cent, but she calmly explained you cannot change another person, but you can always change yourself. Blaming someone outside of your thinking is like blaming your mother for your own unhappiness NOW.

Therefore, Alita chose the wise road. She simply let go of her temper and angry thoughts. She knew she would never fight with her ex-husband again. As the years passed, the two talked and talked, but never once did they even come close to an angry confrontation, because it takes two to fight. Alita had surrendered her anger and replaced it with compassion. He never fully experienced or saw the change, but Alita felt it. Her son was the melting pot between the two parents because they truly loved their youngest child. In the years to come, Alita and her ex-husband grew to experience peaceful feelings with each other, and he learned to give up some of his stubbornness, not because she suggested it, but because it was in the best interests of their son. Later, he mellowed with life, and regained much of his earlier equilibrium.

Interestingly, over the first couple of years of the separation, her ex-husband and son constantly fought over anything and everything, similar to their past relationship. Now, Alita expertly guided her son into loving his father, and when the time came for her son to move into her apartment, he reluctantly, but wisely gave in. The moment the Dad allowed his son the freedom to make his own decisions, the fighting between the two of them subsided, and optimistic feelings in the son replaced anger. Alita had learned to guide her in the direction of love and understanding, but it was her son who chose to walk in that direction.

The key lesson learned was powerful. Thought is an omnipotent vehicle, and if one uses it unwisely, one must pay the price via personal suffering. Once Alita gave up her ugly, angry thoughts, her persona softened and her beauty re-appeared.

As she recollected this time in her life, she thought to herself, "This is a story of *hope*, if only others could hear it."

Chapter 8
Love After the Divorce

Alita had grown comfortable with her life, even though she had not loved a man for many years; however, this was about to change.

In Winnipeg, during her father's funeral ceremony, an athletic, handsome, and tantalizing man by the name of Chaim (pronounced Hi-em) had searched her out, having been touched by Alita's vibrant eulogy at the funeral. He found himself bewitched by her sparkling eyes, vibrant smile and relaxed openness. He instantly felt a sexual attraction to her raw beauty and dark skinned sensuality, for Alita's confidence expressed itself in more ways than just in conversation.

His fun loving nature, youthful vitality and sincerity surprised her. She assumed he would be similar to many Jewish men she had met; talkative, enjoy a good debate, and their Jewish customs (to her) seemed to lean towards being ritualistic and devoid of spiritual essence. To her pleasant surprise, Chaim was alive with Hashem (pronounced Ha-shem, which is the Hebrew word for Creator or God). His eyes expressed an undeniable desire for her and she was drawn to his magnetism. She found stirring inside her a desire to touch the bobbing curls of his black flowing hair.

But, unfortunately, her time in Winnipeg was ending, and upon flying back to Vancouver she returned to the routine which had become her life. Not surprisingly, Chaim phoned and began talking about his mother, who was frail, ridden with sickness and on the edge of death. Alita shared her many feelings surrounding the recent death of her father, and then the two became totally consumed in a three hour long discussion on spirituality. Chaim commented on how close he felt to Alita, as if they had been lifelong friends. Alita concurred, feeling a warm connection. Her heart began to soar like an eagle. Here was the best fish in the pond and she wanted him.

Over the next month of phone calls, their feelings for each other escalated. Every evening, the two talked for hours. At first, the two seemed worlds apart. He described himself as a free spirit, but a Jew who leans towards orthodox rituals and a passion for the entire written work of the Torah (Torah, which are the five books of the Law of Moses; Neveniem, which are the books of the Prophets; and Chetuviem, which are the books of Writings. All these books are brought together under one cover titled Tenach). On investigating the possibilities of a long-term relationship, Chaim insisted they would have to live a Jewish life, which involved a kosher lifestyle, celebrating Shabbat, going to synagogue on a regular basis, and he even mentioned the possibility of her conversion to Judaism. There was to be no compromise on these points. He needed his 'ties or hooks' to his People and their Jewish ways. Alita listened as quietly as possible to these requests. She continued to talk about Great Spirit, while he talked about Hashem; it was undeniable to both of them they were talking about the same Spiritual Creator.

While he insisted that Alita could not meet his criteria for a wife, it did not seem to matter, as they quickly became absorbed in the feelings of love. His spontaneity was stimulating to Alita. He insisted on her saying "I love you," and that it must be meant.

As their long distance love relationship developed, many of the cultural and religious differences seemed to evaporate into thin air. Originally, Alita had felt quite a strong aversion to the Jewish religion; it initially felt cold and intellectual to her. But now, she could not help but be impressed with the softness and fullness of Chaim's rewards in pursuing his Jewish ness. And then, just as Chaim had predicted, Alita began to be drawn into its beauty and wisdom. To her pleasant surprise, the Jewish faith included another aspect besides Torah, which fascinated her— Jewish mysticism or the Kabbalah. These teachings seemed directly connected to Native spirituality, the Tree of Life, and even more specifically, her understanding of the connection between Mind and Spirit. To Alita, the Kabbalah provided proof of the timelessness of the wisdom of Sages.

As described, their feelings of love initially concentrated on discussions of spirituality, centering on Chaim's understanding of the Torah and the Jewish way of thinking, when all of a sudden, the heavens opened!

One day, while the two were on the telephone, she began expressing her love for him, when *the Power of Hashem poured into her soul like a big hand driving its hand down her throat*—she was powerless, she was dead silent and unable to utter a word—Chaim was experiencing exactly the same sensation—*DEAD SILENCE*, which lasted for over five minutes. The stillness became overpowering, eerie and heavenly. It appeared Hashem was connecting their individual spirits into one—like a doctor re-connecting two separated Siamese twins; they were being spiritually joined in total, forceful silence.

Finally, after what seemed an eternity, Chaim regained his power to talk, and said, "Holy Shit, Alita, I am laying on a couch in the living room, it was totally dark, and now there is Light everywhere. I can't believe it. It is so heavenly."

Alita's heart and soul soared, as did Chaim's, by this connection into One Mind and One Heart.

Over the next couple of months the talks over the telephone were always sensuous and full of passion, with many hours talking about if and how they would develop a permanent relationship together. Alita expressed her feelings for him in this poem.

The Magic of Love

My Love for Chaim
is like a dozen roses sitting
on his Shabbat table,
each rose representing
a different
special feeling of my heart.

When asked, what is more special
Being loved or loving one,
My heart answers
Being Loved
but without Loving
One cannot feel the being loved.

When One asks what is Special
about Chaim,
My heart says,
He is true to his heart and knows how to love,
When One asks why is that Special
about Chaim,
My heart says,

HAROLD S. DERBITSKY

Because he is irreplaceable, and
I am the lucky One.

My love is like a red rose,
Each day another petal shines forth,
Each day, my appreciation for what you are
Increases!
If I ever doubt,
Remember
I love you.

From a woman who is learning to love,
Alita

Chapter 9
The Feelings of Love

Chaim's financial life was degenerating, and his pessimism was rampant. To relax his mind, he jumped on his bike and rode to the Red River in Winnipeg. His mind continued to churn as he gazed at the pale slate-colored steady flowing windy river and the cloudy gray sky, for it had rained a few hours earlier. When his eyes shifted to the right he caught sight of a bright shaft of light shining through the clouds. The sunbeam bathed a treed Jutland, which was surrounded by the quiet flowing pale gray river. As he relaxed and took in nature's beauty, a grand rainbow appeared, pouring out and through the many shaped clouds. Four colors were evident—pulsating pink, animated yellow and expansive turquoise which melted into a lingering blue. It captured his attention and took his mind to a far away place, one in which his thoughts no longer existed.

He experienced wave upon wave of contentment, the massive power of Nature pouring into his soul. He drifted in his thoughts and when he found himself back from wherever he had been, he looked at his watch and saw it was now a half-hour later. Refreshed, he jumped on his bike and rode home. For the first time he had learned worry was the human way of complaining, and when his worries were quieted, he felt like a tuna fish freeing itself from a fisherman's hook.

Now, he felt alive and thought of his abounding love for Alita.

At the identical moment, Alita was on her computer and wrote:

Love for My Darling

Love is like a red rose,
pouring its petals
onto the surface of the pond,
shattering the stillness
with tenderness and pleasure.

Our hearts are oceans,
wild with passion and expression.
Feeling the heart of another ocean
is more than words can describe,

for it is LOVE,
and it is the love
I feel for you.

Magically, Chaim telephoned immediately after the last word of her poem was written. Like a little child, she happily read her new love sonnet to him—both enjoyed the tenderness.

They talked randomly and with tenderness for about forty-five minutes. Chaim had casually commented that each time he and Alita talked, it was a totally unique experience, as if Alita transformed into another person each and every time.

"Obviously, because we are in love, we are sensitive to the different moods of each other. In our case, sometimes we experience exactly the same feelings, other times my happiness lifts your spirits, and then other times, you lift and guide me" was Alita's response.

Just before saying good night, Alita began to tell a story and he fell asleep while they were still on the telephone, as his day had been long and tiring. As he awoke, they shared a great laugh and Alita chuckled to herself saying, "Boy, I was really into that story, and you weren't even there." Even that felt good, having a cherished lover to share her life with.

Then, contentedly they wished each other a good night sleep, each saying, "Thanks for being in my life."

Chapter 10
The End of the Telephone Conversations

Alita knew in her heart they had to get together, as over three months had now passed. The feelings between the two were remarkable. This oneness was divine love and each intuitively grasped what the other was feeling most of the time. It was heavenly light, which was lifting their spirits and allowing them to explore the most genuine feelings of love in their hearts.

The sexual energy between the two had become electric. Sometimes, it was as if they were having sex, even though there was very little talk about the intimate act itself. It was not telephone sex, it was natural expressions of sexual feelings, which permeated or originated because they loved each other. Many times Alita slept feeling Chaim was right beside her, and as amazing as it might sound, they almost always knew what the other person was feeling before they telephoned.

Because of this, Alita sensed Chaim was a little afraid of them coming together, so she wrote him an e-mail:

Hi Sweetie:

I am really looking forward to seeing you, and going to the synagogue with you. May our hearts open up to the magic of love. Thanks for being in my life.

Your honey,
Alita

Now, since Alita had saved enough money for a trip to Winnipeg, she and Chaim agreed on a date. Answers would be given, questions resolved, and both would have a much clearer picture of whether they wanted to spend the rest of their lives together—this, to Alita was the big question, while for Chaim, he secretly had reservations and doubts for various reasons, and actually preferred their relationship from a safe distance away.

As the agreed date approached and Alita was ready to book her flight, strange or unlucky events began to happen, as if the Spirits were trying to send her a message. The first thing to happen was the return-flight she wanted was unavailable; secondly her car broke down; next her computer hard drive became defective and she had to have it replaced; and then her CD player broke down. She received further bad news as one of her contracts, which she was counting on for cash flow, was abruptly cancelled. On top of all of these upsets she had to visit the dentist with regard to a problematic tooth and before she knew it, she wasn't able to go—her money had been spent.

Chaim said he would not help her.

This disappointment proved challenging, and her mood dipped.

The following day, her mind flooded with unpleasant thoughts about Chaim, so she simply switched to pleasing thoughts hoping they would guide her back inside to a wise feeling. *'Change your mind, change your mind and change your mind'* became her mantra for the day, and it worked like a charm.

The series of events continued. The next day, when Chaim phoned, he was obviously uncomfortable. He hesitantly revealed he was still married, that he had not mentioned this before because he was afraid he would lose her. He stated he and his wife lived under different roofs and in his mind, they were no longer married. He even felt she would be comfortable in Alita's presence. Alita's heart beat faster as she listened to these admissions. Their future had suddenly grown in complication and uncertainty, but personally she felt no misgivings towards him. She had always prided herself on being tolerant, and truthfully, she had seen much of this same situation in her own community.

In her explanations to her friends about this issue, it drew animated discussions, most often ending with advice to be extremely careful, especially from the women. Several of her friends leaned towards advising her to end the relationship, sometimes with adamant force and/or laughter. None of her friends totally believed such a relationship would last. However all could not deny the power of the love Alita described, and also recognized the intoxication of the power of romance.

Frozen in Time

She realized she was intensely in love with this man who brought so much into her life—the nightly phone calls continued.

One night, once again, they experienced the magical space where they became One. *One Mind, One God, One Thought* had reemerged. Alita had goose bumps and could actually feel the electricity coursing through their bodies.

Chaim, being equally gifted at seeing this Oneness, said "This is unbelievable!" They stayed in this feeling for over an hour; Chaim being fueled by Alita's intoxicating essence. He just loved being in this celestial feeling; it allowed his heart to soar. Alita softly whispered to Chaim that this was Hashem.

She felt so safe with him, and asked if he felt the same way— his answer was a weak kneed "Yes," and the love flowed for all eternity between them.

She began consciously breathing into the telephone, her breath electrifying him, and then she metaphysically pulled him to her—he asked what she was doing and as she explained her sexual feelings, he said, "That's what I thought" and smiled.

This powerful experience made Alita realize she had to be with Chaim as soon as possible. She felt the tightness in the pit of her stomach and the dryness at the back of her throat, and knew she was moist between her legs. Chaim experienced the pressing bulge between his legs, and pleasurably smiled again.

Consequently, after this ethereal experience, they both continued to search the Internet for bargain tickets. Magically one day, a discount airline was practically giving away round trip Vancouver to Winnipeg tickets. The flight was quickly paid for and booked.

Their telephone talks became shorter and full of anticipation. Needless to say, it was more difficult on Chaim. Alita would be coming into his world and his world was in rebellion, but there was no denying his desire. His need to take care of his extensive and time consuming business commitments, his need to balance his old life with the introduction of Alita to his friends, and his own questions in his mind about the relationship were stressful.

However, he was fascinated by the intrigue of having Alita with him again.

Time stopped, but crept forward moment by moment for Alita, each passing moment meant they were that much closer to seeing each other. All life was seen in relation to the moment when she would be on the plane. It seemed forever until the time would come, yet each night meant one day less before the union would be experienced.

He began to fret...

Chapter 11
The Trip

The Beginning

Her sister met her at the airport, and then drove them directly to the festive Canada Day celebration on Osborne Street in Winnipeg; of which Chaim was the organizer. At this celebration, there were many booths selling perfumes, clothes, jewelry and crafts. Music was playing in the distance, and thousands of Winnipeggers were milling around on the streets. The excitement and noise was contagious, aided by the sunny and unexpected warm weather.

Upon meeting up with Chaim, it was obvious to Alita he was not enjoying himself. To Alita he looked ninety years old, burned out and tired, over serious, and worst of all, he was bossy. "There is no room for me in this today," Alita thought. She had expected wild, passionate kisses, feelings of love and amour, and the two of them desiring to be together. What happened was the opposite.

So she excused herself from this carnival setting, which upset him even more, and her sister drove the two of them to her home. For the next two days, she poured her heart and mind into enjoying all her family. She realized Chaim and her might never come together on this trip, for he was obsessed with the frantic pace of his life, and seemed incapable of slowing down to include a few hours of peace and tenderness with Alita.

She appreciated Chaim was a treasure in her life; he had taught her heart how to love again in a more spontaneous and passionate way than she had ever experienced before. Therefore, he deserved, in her mind, every chance in the world to experience the beauty and full potential of their relationship, and this would include their eyes meeting and their hands actually touching and caressing each other's body.

Her understanding of the mystical world of the Spirit had taught her well. Why waste time dwelling on a million disappointing thoughts (for in this wisdom she escaped all the misery that would trap most human beings in similar circumstances)? This patience allowed her to enjoy her holiday, even though it had very uncomfortable elements in its fiber.

Shabbat

For six days you may perform melachah (On Shabbath, Jews are permitted to do melachah (work) that isn't laborious and the only melachah they are permitted to perform are those related to food preparation), but the seventh day is a complete Shabbat, holy to the LORD…it is an eternal sign that in six days, the LORD made heaven and earth, and on the seventh day he rested and was refreshed….Exodus 31:15-17

Luckily, Shabbat (Saturday, the weekly Jewish holy day) was approaching. Chaim and Alita had discussed over the telephone how wonderful it would be to spend much of these twenty-six hours together, beginning with Shabbat dinner on Friday night.

Shabbat began at sundown on Friday; Chaim's house exploded with activity. Astonishingly delicious smelling kosher foods were being prepared. Chaim, while stressed at times, was obviously happy in his element, enjoying the familiar and ritualistic activities of the evening. His wife, who was surprisingly there, appeared relaxed, performing an integral part of the preparations. Fifteen of Chaim's Jewish relatives and friends along with Alita sat at the beautifully laid table.

After dovining (praying) and lighting the Shabbat candles, everyone sat around the large oval table, with Chaim and his mother next to each other, his wife at opposite ends, and Alita at mid table. Two Challahs (Jewish braided egg bread) and red wine sat on the table. Chaim began the ceremony with the breaking of the bread, which was lightly salted. Everyone tasted a small piece of the Challah and drank wine from the communal cup as it was passed around, while Hebrew prayers were joyfully and enthusiastically delivered. Chaim's wise mother then prayed; the room felt sacred and holy as it filled with the mother's insightful words.

Finally, the dinner arrived and was placed on the beautifully set table, and the buzz of a contented crowd grew. Alita could only marvel at the many courses so beautifully prepared. She had never tasted such delicious food in all her life. In her mind it was better than the finest restaurants. The dinner was highlighted by kosher prime rib which Alita could not stop eating. It was so succulent, tender and cooked to perfection. It was also unbelievably expensive, which kosher foods tend to be.

To her pleasant surprise, Chaim started to smile and relax with his mother, wife and crowd of Jewish friends. This was his element. He took Shabbat as a holy day, where smiles, joy and relaxed laughter were key elements. Alita was impressed. His face certainly looked different when he smiled, and the years rolled off his face. He enjoyed sharing the Shabbat feeling with his community of friends. Alita always respected this feeling of community, as it is inherent and natural in her own people. The evening rolled on and proved to be a cultural and social delight.

As agreed upon by them, early the next morning, Alita strolled over to his house, as Chaim's religious beliefs did not allow the driving of a car on Shabbat. This was to be the beginning of their first date, which would open with a quiet walk to the synagogue. It was a most pleasant walk, with the weather accommodating their mood, gorgeous small bushed trees danced before their eyes, and architecturally built houses, each one more interesting than the last, set a wonderful tone of preparation for the two love birds. Alita found the synagogue service to be reasonably interesting. After the service, she briefly talked to the smiling rabbi. This did not provide any new insights for Alita, but there was still magic to be experienced later on at the synagogue.

A delightful lunch and an optional one-hour Torah class always followed the Shabbat service in this synagogue. In this class, Alita was allowed to express her mind. This group of fifteen shared thought-provoking revelations and observations. To her amazement and surprise, Chaim talked about levels of consciousness, from a feeling which could only be described as original and profound. Alita felt hope spring into her heart, and complimented him on what he had expressed.

On their walk home, they held hands for the first time, and this felt wonderful. The rest of Shabbat was peacefully spent together.

The Final Day

While the remainder of her stay was unpredictable, the final day proved to be the most eventful. In the week that had passed, the couple had shared some occasional intimate moments and many rough patches, as the reality of physically being together proved considerably more challenging than talking on the telephone.

The final day had started almost like the first day, with its indecisiveness and irritabilities. Chaim telephoned three times trying to arrange their schedule, and as Alita waited patiently and quietly for him to come, he managed to discover many different excuses not to be there. This was particularly disappointing as she felt the moment was full of Hawaiian mana (magic)[5].

She sat on the steps of her sister's home. Blooming mums, yellow and pink bellcups, pansies, vibrant grasses and various peaceful sights greeted her. The birds were chirping, the sky was cloudy, but the air felt warm and balmy to the skin. What a treat! Chaim was out doing whatever he needed to do and she was alone, sitting in tranquility. Although many will not understand how Alita achieved this state of mind, she had come to realize she was fine. Her thoughts continued, "This trip was rolling to an end and life had not stopped. Tomorrow she would be back in Vancouver. One more evening in Winnipeg; who knows what it would bring? She smiled, thinking Chaim would be his usual unpredictable self, and she was going to accept and flow with it. They might never be the couple she dreamed about, as she sighed. No sense in ruining a great last twelve hours in Winnipeg with unfulfilled expectations—not one of them had come true and yet she was blessed with many loving feelings. She was BLESSED indeed!"

When Chaim finally arrived he was in a dither, but as the planned evening with her sister and relatives progressed into coffee and a pastry at an exquisite hotel, he began to relax. The Fort Garry Hotel was a majestic, grand old hotel, more like one would find in Europe rather than in Winnipeg. The elegant dining room steeped of history and opulence. The softness of their feelings began to explode in this romantic atmosphere. They softly touched each other hands, while the pianist played his soft alluring songs of love. Intimacy was growing and Alita was enjoying herself, as she realized there was no sense in holding back her feelings on their last night.

They had shared some beautiful, sensual and intimate feelings the previous night. Now at last, a young-hearted Chaim wanted to spend the final night alone with her. She was pleasantly surprised it actually was going to happen as they entered a posh hotel room.

There they were, he was looking into her eyes, and they shone with a quiet sereneness. He felt she looked exactly like an eagle—regal, confident, and yet so mystical. He felt he had never seen anything so beautiful. How could this amazing human being be in front of him! He experienced this voluptuous and sensuous being, a mystical goddess who was this amazing teacher. She guided him to slow down and listen to what she was expressing from her heart. These expressions were not with words, but with subtlety.

He felt a spiritual energy coming out of his mouth—like millions of bits of energy pieces deep-rooted inside him, calling to her, and she responded, their tongues coming together in a dance of love, their bodies pulled together and then what they experienced could only be described as a dance of Oneness, and what harlequin romance novels revel in and attempt to describe. Here was perfection, for together their sexual wisdom united in a softness that was beyond exciting—it was their life forces joining as One.

Leaving Winnipeg

As she sat on the airplane, Alita's first thoughts where that she could live without Chaim, because the week had been so disappointing. After a short nap and resting her mind, the amorous and sensual feelings of the night before poured into her being. She realized she was even more intensely in love with Chaim than before the trip. She did not know what would come, but her desire for Chaim's body, his mind and spirit was grabbing at her very soul.

These feelings grew over the next few days, yet there was also a sense of freedom. She had grown more in love, yet more detached. Her thoughts were of enjoyment and undeniable sexual feelings for Chaim, yet she knew her Winnipeg time had left her more as an observer, as well as an actor in this romantic play that was headlining her life.

Her sacred understandings had saved her from being devoured by her raw physical feelings for Chaim, and her dreams of a union. Chaim unconsciously would have dominated and controlled her, being the person he was. Sacred knowledge protects those who understand it. She was not devoured by his weaknesses; she was now allowed to taste all his goodness, specialness and magical gifts that were contained within him. These were immense. In fact, she had more respect for him than ever, for he had this aliveness and an amazing passion for life. He was both confident and sensitive in guiding her to the secrets of life and love.

Love does not devour us. Sex does not control us. Relationships are not meant to be obsessive. No aspect of life dominates us, unless we let it. We seek a balance to life—of enjoying positive feelings while not being devoured or enticed by feelings of insecurity.

Because of the knowledge she acquired from her visit to Winnipeg, she saw herself sitting in insecure emotions without being bothered by them. As she objectively observed this new understanding, she saw this inner calmness had changed her destiny. She understood the Great Spirit or Hashem had guided them through a most remarkable experience. In Alita's mind, the only way to describe this miracle was to call it 'God's expression of Light and Truth'.

Now, if only Chaim could quiet his busy mind!

Chapter 12
Reflections after the Trip

Alita's Reflections

It is easy to feel sorry for ourselves when we encounter another's weaknesses, but Hashem has a purpose. Alita found she had fallen madly in love with Chaim, and his magnetic physical presence. He had become transformed from an old man into the most handsome and magnetic man she had ever encountered. She could not believe that anyone could look that enticing and captivating; she could easily have worshipped this physical Adonis. However, after experiencing his weaknesses, this served as a protection against being overwhelmed and/or overindulging in passion or lust. As gorgeous as he was, the essence of their relationship was the metaphysical, not the physical, and the essence of their relationship revolved around them growing, not remaining stationary.

Somehow the weaknesses meant growth, and she realized Chaim might want to change. She would wait to see if Chaim had experienced the healing power of love, which would change him forever, and quiet his mind in a way he had never experienced before.

Alita remembered at the Torah class talking to an elderly Jewish lady about life and death being a continuum, whereby after death, humans re-enter their new life as a baby with exactly the same level of consciousness in which they had died. The lady had commented it is too bad we cannot remember our previous life experiences. Alita mentioned this was probably for the best; for if we could remember previous lives, it would probably demoralize us with trials and tribulations. Much like looking into the future and if we knew what lay ahead, we would never venture in that direction because of all the heartache one would experience. Yet when we do and arrive at the end of the journey, we are wiser and more appreciative of what life has to offer us. This is how Alita felt about Chaim.

Chaim's Reflections

His level of understanding had grown, and in the next week's Torah class, he noticed the members of the class did not grasp what he was talking about. They were taking the biblical stories literally, and he was suggesting they look more profoundly, and to his unpleasant surprise, they would not. When Alita asked him whether he noticed he had jumped a level of consciousness, he said, "No, I just feel more secure and am able to talk more clearly and succinctly about things which I always knew." Alita laughed to herself as he had just defined, in his own words, *a heightened state of consciousness.*

Now, she wondered if this would translate into him being more secure in their relationship.

Chapter 13
The Second Date

One and a half months had passed since the visit to Winnipeg. Initially, the love between them had continued to grow. However, lately it had slowed and become a bit stagnant, especially once the new dates for her two-week stay in Winnipeg had been set. Chaim expressed how wonderful a second coming together would be, however, Alita sensed he was not certain about this trip. She could feel the distance growing between them.

This cooler feeling seemed to expand over the forthcoming weeks. Chaim became more distant. She was also having some difficulty comprehending she was again heading toward Winnipeg. She knew the Creator had given them a gift, but she could only describe this trip as 'unknown'.

Finally the day arrived, her flight was taken and she arrived in Winnipeg. Chaim and her sister were there to meet her, but once again he was remote and scared, much like the beginning of her first trip.

While she enjoyed many highlights, there were many disappointing times with Chaim. She felt occasional intimate moments, and as beautiful as they were, they were quashed by many awkward and uncomfortable times. The love was still there, but once again, even more extremely than the first visit; they seemed to have become two lost souls missing each other. She was not as settled and secure as before, and she experienced some loneliness. She also found Chaim was even more controlling and competitive than before.

Alita began mentioning the possibility that their relationship could not continue as before and Chaim seemed oblivious to these talks and was convinced they would continue their relationship over the telephone once she returned to Vancouver.

On the last night together she told him their relationship was over. This had shocked him, but she was convinced this was the best for both of them. What had brought about this feeling was a realization Chaim would not alter his life in any shape or form, and even more importantly, would not spend intimate times alone with her. She began to realize he had loving feelings for her, but could not give her what she so desperately needed, and without this, it left her wanting. Perhaps, Alita surmised, he had experienced his fill of happiness in the relationship.

The trip closed without the intimacy of a final night together, without a positive ending and with the finality of everyone in Winnipeg thinking the relationship was over.

However, she found upon returning to Vancouver that she slipped into uncomfortable emotions, and realized she missed him in her life. So she telephoned. They made up very easily as he had missed her as well, stating how surprised he was by how much this separation had hurt.

However, now there was a different composition or shift in their relationship. Because while talking on the telephone, feelings of intimacy were experienced, but, after hanging up, Alita now understood they had different assumptions about their relationship. Deep in his soul, from the beginning, Chaim intuitively always knew the relationship would never fully work out. He still treasured and wanted the existing telephone relationship to continue as it gave him sustenance and revitalized him. No other person had touched his heart in this manner. In a way, Chaim wanted his cake and eat it too.

Chapter 14
The Bittersweet

Whether the relationship could work out began to be a constant puzzle in Alita's mind. They had tasted the fruit of love, the pleasure of experiencing each other, and as always, it is better to have loved and lost rather than avoid love. When writing to a friend, Alita described the relationship as melodramatic and bittersweet. It meant so much to her to share an experience of love with another, to taste the sweetness of a mate, and to dream of coming together.

Did she still love Chaim? As much as she now did not want to love him, she always would. Yet, in a bittersweet way, she knew they would never be lovers again. He simply did not realize there are windows of opportunity or special moments in the history of a relationship, and his failure to grasp her intimate needs was at the root of their breakup. And this is not to say, that Alita had not been guilty of the same, for she realized this was one of the causes of her divorce—her own failure to grasp the intimate needs of her husband.

"Could Chaim have been different or could the ending have been different?" she wondered. It turns out these are irrelevant questions. They were not to be together, and never would be again. This bittersweet realization freed Alita to begin walking anew. In her heart, the beauty and tenderness of Chaim would always remain tucked away.

Later, Alita met with her sister in Vancouver and talked about her relationship with Chaim, and why they were no longer together. Alita expressed it like this, "When you go to an incredible restaurant, and the food is absolutely delicious, but the plate has very little on it like a thin piece of scrumptious meat, a delectable one-quarter potato and no vegetables, and the cost is five hundred dollars, some people come away from that restaurant saying, 'It was not enough, there simply was not enough food for the cost'. Despite the quality of the meal, they are left wanting and unfulfilled. That is how I ended up seeing Chaim and myself. And so it ended, even though Chaim would have been totally satisfied to continue our relationship at that level forever. Another person may have made a different decision, but I have reached peace with mine.

While life is sometimes incredibly difficult, it does open our hearts to the next oncoming spiritual experiences, if we want them. The way to 'want them' is to raise our eyes to the sky and watch our thoughts soar to the heavens."

Later, Alita wrote this poem:

As our dance of love
reaches its final destination.
As the magic of the dance
quiets to a still.
As the wonderment of a year past
has floated by.

We recognize two great ships
have sailed to different ports.

Our hearts have been blessed.
But now, the worlds we see
are nay, not together

Yet, we have dreamed and
come together,
and now apart.

With a profound feeling in her heart, and a tear in her eye, Chaim had transformed into an ex-mate and a distant friend. As the last word of the poem was written, her phone rang; and before she knew it, she had agreed to a date with an interesting gentleman!

Post Script—(Reflections)

The Connection Between
Native and Jewish Worlds

Chapter 15
The Wolf

During their past relationship Alita had become aware of Chaim's definite commitment to his faith. Even though Alita was non-religious and non-denominational in her spirituality, she realized in order to be with Chaim, she must come to appreciate the Jewish way of thinking. Chaim was adamant all religions come from Judaism and she was intrigued by this strong assertion from her lover.

Chaim had expressed to those who observe Shabbat, it is a precious gift from God, a day of great joy eagerly awaited for through the week, a time when all weekday concerns are set aside and we devote ourselves to higher pursuits. He added it is the only ritual observance instituted in the Ten Commandments and that Shabbat is primarily a day of rest and spiritual enrichment.

Alita was beginning to appreciate the sacred nature of this day of rest, so when the sun set on the Friday evening, she lit a candle in her apartment in honor of Hashem, and prayed as Chaim had taught her. Early Saturday, she reflected and experienced the blessing of sacred thoughts, which had poured into her heart from the previous evening's prayers. Thanks to these reflections, the day expressed itself like a babbling brook flowing into its mother river.

Alita attended Black Fox's sweat lodge on many Saturday afternoons. At 3:00 p.m. she made her way down to the sweat. The fire was blazing as usual. She carefully tossed some of her sacred medicines and tobacco into the hot fire as she prayed to the four symbolic directions of North, South, East and West. She realized she had not brought her drum, but today she thought she might not need it. This proved true, as the drum would have been a distraction for what she was about to experience.

The day was sunny, and the sweat would be crowded, as a group of fifteen to twenty people had come to join in. As Alita crawled into the spot pointed out to her by the Pourer of the Water, she consciously quieted her mind. She had come for a reason. She wanted to be taken to the beginning of time when humans and her own spirit began living on Mother Earth. Medicines were thrown on the hot river lava rocks and she inhaled the exotic aromas. The lodge was closed into darkness, and then the rocks were splashed with water.

She asked or prayed for the time before the beginning of Judaism. Almost immediately an apparition appeared. Alita's mouth opened widely and she growled, "Aaaaaahhhhhhhhhhh" savagely, with her jaw and teeth moving back and forth in weird contortions. In front of her appeared a wildly savage mouth with sharp, jagged teeth, saliva feverishly poured off its teeth and gums. It had a long snout, it was wild and terrifying—it was a Spiritwolf or a wolf-man, and it frightened her. She calmed her fright as quickly as she could and felt the spirit walk into her calmer being. She found herself growling, her mouth was savagely open and saliva streamed down her lips. This animal spirit and she were joining! Her widely opened mouth had become that of the Spiritwolf—an actual wolf transporting her into the wolf spirit world. This experiential and spiritual vision continued for about five minutes, its presence and power remaining within her for the whole sweat. She became this savage, terrifying, raw beast. This, she experienced was already a part of her true nature and being reminded of it felt useful and valuable. She felt strong and she was a wolf.

Later, she visited Grey Wolf, an adopted and wise member of the wolf clan, and he confirmed this was the second sighting of this spirit. He validated it was a good spirit, that it would tell her what she wanted, but she would have to ask and believe in what she asked and was told. This spirit wanted to help her.

Leaving Grey Wolf, she felt a warm wave of contentment pour into her. This was a good omen. Life was opening up to her, and she was fascinated by its spiritual possibilities.

The next day as she meditated by a quiet stream in the forest, this interpretation flowed into her:

'The wolf spirit was her spirit from the beginning of time for this was her clan. Somehow, not clearly seen at this time, she was connected to the Jewish People via the Wolf People. In some way, both their ancestors linked her and Chaim. Maybe even a prehistoric wolf woman found a Jewish man as a mate and simply evolved into a Jewish way of thinking.'

She remembered a story about 'Thought' from one of her Elders.

An Elder Cherokee Native American was teaching his grandchildren about life.

He said to them, "A fight is going on inside all humans, it is a terrible fight and it is between two wolves.

One wolf represents fear, anger, envy, sorrow, regret, greed, arrogance, self-pity, resentment, inferiority, lies, false pride, superiority and ego.

The other stands for joy, peace, love, hope, sharing, serenity, humility, kindness, benevolence, friendship, empathy, generosity, truth, compassion and faith.

This same fight is going on inside you, and inside every other person, too."

They thought about it for a minute and then one child asked her grandfather, "Grandpa, which wolf will win?"

The old Cherokee simply replied, **"The one you feed."**

Chapter 16

Kabbalah and Torah

As Alita began to take an interest in Jewish history, she learned the Jewish People were directly connected to the Torah or the Old Testament. In the Covenant from Mount Sinai, God talked to or through Moses. In Alita's opinion, as time passed, the mystical part of the teachings began to lose their importance to the Jewish People. They appeared to take the Covenant as a personal possession rather than God's mystical gift that exists in all human beings. In her mind, the Christian People were the same.

When she attended synagogue with Chaim, her appreciation and respect for the Torah grew. Whenever she went to a service, she would often take time to read excerpts from the book of the Torah. It seemed every paragraph expressed a similar message.

All life is Spiritual.
We, as Spiritual Beings, are either moving
towards God's Greatness,
or
away from it.

In Alita's mind, human beings have a role in their relationship with God. They must plant the seeds of their thoughts in fertile soil, and then God or Great Spirit will bring the garden alive via fragrant and lovely flowers, as long as we water the flowers and remove the weeds. Removing the weeds would be symbolic to quieting negative or doubting thoughts, and watering would be our faith. With faith and a quiet mind, we walk in 'heaven here on earth', Alita recalled from an Elder's teachings.

The above can be expressed in a million different ways, and that is why we have so many different religions that describe the same God from different perspectives, beliefs and rituals. However, should one religion approach the Light from a different angle, it does not mean that the final goal and destination are not the same, for after all, there is only One God.

For example, Alita remembered in a sweat, a woman asked the leader of the sweat for Spirit guidance as to what type of employment she should be doing. The answer she received from the Wise man of the sweat was she must make her own decision as to what direction she wanted to work towards and the Spirits would be there to help her in whatever decision she made.

Kabbalah[6]

Chaim felt committed to the Torah or Old Testament, but he also studied the Kabbalah, which he described as the inner meaning of Torah and the two cannot be separated. As he began explaining the Kabbalah or Jewish mysticism, which originated from the time of Eden, Alita noticed how similar it was to Native mysticism. First, there was a Tree of Life, which is a mystical concept within the Kabbalah to understand the nature of God. For the Native People the Sacred Medicine Wheel is the Sacred

Tree of Life and is used to provide purpose and understanding in the lives of human beings and their relationship to the Creator. Then she remembered the Jewish word for God was 'Hashem', while her Coast Salish People said 'Asem'. The sounds were so similar; in her mind she felt they must have originated from the same beginning. Even being Jewish felt like being Native. Both are more than cultures or religions, and both are intuitively comfortable with their own clan.

While in Winnipeg, Alita attended a ceremony in a synagogue (a Jewish house of prayer). She watched with curiosity as the great scrolls of Torah were lifted out of a large rectangular wooden cabinet and spread open in front of a serene male, who then began reading to the congregation in clear Hebrew diction. What caught Alita's fascination were the symbols of decoration on the tapestry that surrounded the cabinet (The scrolls are kept in a cabinet in the synagogue called an "ark," as in Ark of the Covenant). The tapestry had many animals on it—a lion, donkey, wolf, deer with antlers and various others. After the ceremony was completed, she went up to the Rabbi and asked him what the significance of the animals is? He said each animal represents the different Jewish tribes. "Do you mean like the Native Indians do with their clans and totems?" responded Alita.

The Rabbi grinned and quickly stated, "Just remember we were first."

Alita laughed and smiled to herself, saying 'Hmmmmm, I wonder'. She secretly began to speculate about the possibility of the early Aboriginals having joined or established a coalition with the Israelites, and possibly later becoming one or all of the ten long lost tribes of Israel. In her further research on the topic, she discovered a theory the early residents of the Americas were actually descended from the tribe of Joseph. No archeological proof has ever been found[4].

Later, Chaim had discussed with Alita about the first three (Keter, Chohmah, Binah) of the ten Sefirahs (divine emanations of light) in the Kabbalah, saying they described the three primary elements of the Mind. He mentioned a major theme of the Kabbalah is *'God is all, all is God'*.

Alita thought to herself, "Just like the teachings of my Elders."

Later, Alita met a very wise Rabbi, who told her about Das (the Spirit defined as unspeakable and impossible to describe). "All a rabbi or any spiritual teacher can do is to describe Das in the form of a metaphor. For example, using the metaphor of attempting to describe a bottomless hole—the best one could do would be to describe 'the rim' of the hole. If the rabbi keeps describing the rim around the hole, perhaps one day the student will accidentally fall into the indescribable hole, and experience the essence of God.

This is the same as any sage trying to describe Universal Truth or a person in love describing Love to someone who has never been in love. Similarly, this can be the same with religion; many of the believers are confused because God is impersonal, yet our experience of God is personal."

Chapter 17
Healing of Heart and Mind

*"You know that wolves must be with humans, and that otherwise
humans will destroy too much?"*
...Dorthy Hearst, "Promise of the Wolves"

As Alita sat with others in the sweat, she began to talk:

"There was an interesting Shoshone woman named
Sacajawea[7] who accompanied Lewis and Clarke on their great
adventures across the United States. "As the blood had begun to
swim between her legs, Sacajawea's ceremony for womanhood
was held. She was taken to sit on a skin in front of the lodge to the
South where the Shaman supervised the raising of the ceremonial
wickiup, singing with the singer as the poles were placed so the
tips inclined until they met in a point at the top. The Shaman
chanted to her, *'Plant a thought, harvest an act.' While others sang, plant
an act, harvest a habit, plant a habit, harvest a character, plant a character,
harvest a destiny."*

Alita commented:

'When you truly heal yourself, then you can help others,
and like the Shaman's chant
Thought has something to do with it."

In my recent pursuits, I came to realize other cultures exists which equally treasures the feeling of family among all their people—for example, the Jewish People. Both the Jewish and the Native people share a feeling of oneness with their own.

It is my belief, at one point in the earliest of times, our original Elders and these other culture's Ancients either worked together or were one together. It is my prayer the time will come, with the help of the Spirits, that all of the tribes of the world will join, once again, in harmony; thus bringing a vision of hope to our worlds. In union, we will learn to grow and live a balanced life.

Obviously, this would be one of my wishes for the whole world, but if our People could enjoy working with other similar valued cultures, then a healing would naturally follow.

As I said, this is my belief and wish for the world.

Section 3

Alita's Dream

Chapter 18
The Vision

The brilliant green waters of the Lillooet River roared in the background, just a few feet away from the cave. Its banks crept sharply down, having claimed many a drunken neighbor or careless child. Coho and sockeye salmon fought the speedy current as they instinctually swam upstream to their spawning grounds. The mighty fifty pound Spring salmon swam deeper down, having enough meat to feed a whole village celebrating the first catch of the season.

Fire crackled in the cave, sparks whirling upward. Along the floor, cedar boughs and dry grass broke the chill seeping from the floor. A smoke-darkened deer hide kept the wind's blasts from penetrating the doorway in the rock. At each quarter of the circle's edge, a Black Bear tooth, Eagle feather, Mouse skin and deer antler carved in the shape of a Buffalo stared at the flickering light—symbols of ancient shaman Power.

As the woman leaned tiredly forward, long tangles of thick black hair tumbled across her face, reflecting a bluish sheen in the fire's glow. Gently, she patted the decaying rock below her feet.

"I'm still here…." she murmured, "waiting. You didn't think I'd gone, did you?"

When no answer came, Alita settled back against the cold stone wall, grumbling irritably to herself. She chanted softly, hands tracing ancient symbols of Spirit Power in the air before her. She plucked a hand full of cedar and dipped it into the weather beaten water bucket sitting to her right. Shaking the cedar branches, she shook some of the water and tossed some cleansing medicines onto the flames. Steam and blaze exploded. Four times she repeated the process, warm wet smoke billowing up to the top of the cavern.

"There," she whispered, eyes probing beyond the smoke tinged walls. "I've heard you calling".

Huddling over the flames, she closed her eyes, the traces of her timeless beauty barely obscured by time. She inhaled four times, allowing peace and tranquility to flow through her like a morning mist awakening a newfound day. The intoxicating odor of the medicines filled her senses.

Four days she had fasted, singing, bathing in the warm waters of the healing hot springs that bubbled up from the earth, steaming in the frigid air beyond the shelter. She had sung, prayed and purged her body of the ills of bad thoughts and wrong deeds.

But in the haze of smoke, still no vision appeared. She hesitated, frightened, feeling the call. Slowly she filled her lungs, exhaling as she looked at the sacred calf-hide bundle. "Yes," she whispered, "I fear your Power," as her heartbeat quickened.

The call came again, tugging at her soul. Alita made her decision. With trembling fingers, she lifted the sacred medicine from her calf skin bag and undid the layers of tied red cloth, displaying four thin pieces of the powerful mushroom. Each of these she passed four times through the warm cedar smoke, once for each of the four directions of the world. East for spiritual renewal, South for the loving emotions of the heart, West for physical strength and North for the dawning of true wisdom and intellectual balance.

One by one, she purified the mushrooms and lifted them to her lips, slowly chewing. Bitterness stung her tongue. She swallowed and leaned back, relaxing into the mysterious zone she was about to enter.

Alita squinted, her ancient eyes trying to focus in the haze of smoke emanating from the fire. Minutes passed as she peered. An image grew in the mist—a casual and rather overpowering smiling man appeared. She looked into her dream for more but there was just this White man. Alita felt confused, "What was he doing in her dream?" She looked again and recognized some mysterious, sacred Power calling her. Her flashing eyes gleamed as she followed the dream—the man entered an ill kept, dilapidated old house on a typical Native reserve. Inside, there was a youth, this time an Indian, and he was sniffing some white powder. Many bottles of beer and whiskey were scattered around the messy abode. Alita felt a sadness that gnawed at her soul. So much suffering in her People and she was powerless to help. Tears rolled down her cheek, as this stifling feeling of caring overpowered her heart.

A kind smile appeared on the mysterious man, as the scene changed to another day in the same setting. Now, the mysterious man was casually talking to the youth, and there was a look of wonderment on the poor Indian's face. Alita recognized something had changed—something wonderful had affected his suffering. She saw it in the youth's sparkling eyes. He suddenly looked rejuvenated; his body and face vibrant with the spiritual energy of newfound hope. What had happened to this youth? She did not fully understand. Did not all answers to the suffering of her People sit in the realm of the Spirit World? The kind non-

Indian man had not performed any ceremony, or even called for the Great Spirit, and yet there was this miraculous transformation.

"White men never really understand Indian People," she thought, but this White man had casually walked into an Indian home and for some surprising reason, she wanted to touch him. Oh, he was alluring! A stir in her womanhood awoke. She became amazed at the magnetic pull of this powerful magician. "What could be the meaning of these strange newfound feelings she was experiencing? Surely, this White fool does not know more than the wisdom of the Elders, or perhaps," thought Alita, "His gift is fresh and alive with newness."

The vision broke, wisps of smoke carrying it up through the rock to the chill night beyond. Alita clenched her hands into fists, feeling the effects of the mushroom. She staggered to her feet, and wobbled past the deer-hide hangings. Frigid night air gripped her as she bent and vomited violently.

The voices of the mushrooms whispered in her blood, mystery in their sultry tones as she struggled to allow the mushroom to fade in her veins. As she blinked and rubbed her mouth, a wolf howled in the night, piercing, tying itself to the vision.

Chapter 19
The Smiling Fool or the Messenger

He was a tall, athletic, rugged looking White man of sixty who traveled freely in the Native Indian world. He exhibited a kind and gentle nature with a bit of a determined exterior, which sometimes hid his heart of gold. His smile awoke childlike feelings in adults, yet when he spoke to them, they were not sure whether he was powerful or just crazy. He seemed to be often found complaining about the weaknesses of the present day Indian thinking, yet some could see great hope in his eyes towards the Indian potential and future. No one doubted he was intelligent and charismatic.

The Gathering

The gathering had begun around 5:00 pm at the Aboriginal Centre, located in the poorer district of the scenic and successful city of Vancouver, Canada. Two hundred urban Natives had arrived for the Wednesday evening dinner and Powwow. Twenty Nisha dancers were to provide the after dinner entertainment with their unique dancing style and drumming. Before dinner, ten random hand drummers had ventured out onto the centre of the hall, drumming and singing familiar songs. The beat was distinct and most in the crowd relaxed to the pleasing melodies of the ancient songs.

The People curiously glanced as a smiling White man dressed in clean jeans, brown cowboy shirt and old weathered baseball cap carrying an ancient looking drum with a large wolf head painted on its deerskin cover, walked over and casually joined the other skilled drummers. He was by no means the best of the drummers or the singers, but none could deny that he fit in, not only in skill to the beat, but most importantly, in his relaxed and comfortable manner. The crowd noted that this White Elder was totally immersed in the drumming and at peace with himself as he listened intently to the beats of the other experienced drummers. He belonged and the People of the gathering were glad.

The drumming continued for one-half hour, then dinner was announced and all saw the great flood of food pour onto the empty tables. The drummers returned their drums to their decorated drum cases, and eagerly wandered to the food. A sharp-eyed Chief of one of the nearby communities had curiously observed the unusual drummer, and with intended purpose, walked over to begin the conversations with him. The Chief asked how he had become comfortable with the Native ways, and the 'smiling fool' looked profoundly into the eyes of the powerful Chief, and told him of some of his experiences with twenty Native communities across British Columbia and Minnesota. Then he casually mentioned that he was looking for someone who would know what he was talking about.

The Chief said, "You are not the smiling fool we might think you are."

He sighed and replied. "I know a little of the plants, of Power, and their uses, that's all. A wiser man would be more powerful, but I am content with my limitations. I can tell you about walking with the Spirit, but I do not want you to listen to my words. My role is simple—I just point to the reality that exists within each and every person in the Universe. Unfortunately, when I talk about this, some People mistakenly believe I know what I am talking about. This is not true. Luckily, we all possess that special knowledge."

The Chief then asked if he had met 'One Who Knows' and he nodded affirmatively. "It is an honor to say 'Yes'."

The Chief continued, "And was he an Indian?"

The messenger smiled, "I have been honored to meet many wise Indian and medicine men/women, all of whom have taught me much about Spirit and its connection to this life. I will always be indebted to them for guiding me to become a better man and in their sharing of the Native Way. However, the 'One Who Knows' was not one of those; his knowledge is beyond all that I have just mentioned and his healing Power unmatched by anyone I have met in this Universe. In fact, his wisdom is so simple, that it is my belief that no one, including myself, has really heard what he is saying. However, the impact on my life for the betterment is undeniable, and the glow of the Spirit Within is much brighter because of my meeting and friendship with this man.

Then, the messenger expressed something that surprised the Chief. "I have talked to 100's of Indians and while they are very keen to teach their great wisdoms and stories of life, they do not want to learn or listen about the *bridge* which we travel on back and forth between the world of Spirit and the world of human suffering. This is a shame because the answer is right in front of their noses.

Now, Great Chief, do you know anyone who would like to listen to my words as well as my drum, or must I travel to another community in search of this elusive target?

"No," the Chief looked with awe into the power he was seeing, "I am not this person you are seeking, for my world is of administration, business and politics, but I am aware of one whom I believe you will be glad to meet. There are many wise men and women, as you are aware in our world, but there is one whom I respect for her open mind. I believe you will enjoy talking to her because she travels equally into the ancient world of the sacred Spirit and the modern world of today's civilization. Some of our People do not trust her. She is called Alita and I know one who will point you towards her direction. Good luck, my friend, and may our paths cross on your return journey."

The messenger nodded with comfort in his eyes as the Chief pointed to a half drunk frail looking wild haired Native sitting by himself in the corner of the gathering.

The 'smiling fool' walked over and sat beside this skinny, sickly looking man with messy hair and wild eyes, who was feverishly gobbling up all the food on his plate. 'The messenger' felt his loneliness and desperate struggles with life, but could sense some latent spiritual power—the man who lived inside this body was invisible to almost all, except a very few.

"Hi, I am Sam, and how are you enjoying the food?"

A friendly smile beamed between a mouth full of turkey and gravy, and sheepishly replied, "I am Jimmy Peters and glad to meet you, Sam. I like your drumming, the more drummers the better. It raises the spirit of the People to hear the old songs, I know it raises mine. I dance at the Longhouse sometimes when I am not too drunk or drugged out."

A bond had quickly been established between the two men and a sense of comfort arose in Jimmy. He began talking about how he had almost kicked his bad habit of drinking with the help of a wise woman. He continued, "She guided me to a quiet and silent place inside myself. She built a sweat lodge where just the two of us sweated. She kept pointing for me to 'go inside to this quiet place' and while she was not interested in Christianity, I often talked about the 'Spirit of Jesus Christ' while the water was being poured on the rocks. I was surprised how strongly I felt about the Christ Spirit. I guess some of my early upbringing stuck.

He smiled, 'Not Christ the man, you know, just Christ Spirit that resides in all of us, whether Indian, White, Muslim, Hindu or Jewish.' This woman was different, and I could almost taste what she talked about. There I was at the threshold of being cured, and then I became cursed and lost it all."

"What do you mean? How were you cursed?"

The answer surprised Sam. "Oh, I got an inheritance of several hundred thousand dollars. I got lost in partying and all that money, immersing myself into drugs; you know the white powder. It was not long before everyone was partying at my newly purchased place, which I luckily bought with some of the money. It was great, I really felt I knew what I was doing and talking about. I bought drugs for everyone and everyone encouraged me and they were my friends and over time the money was gone. This healing lady would occasionally show up at my place, but not stay long.

You know it was strange. Before, when I was not drugging or temporarily clear of the alcohol, I mostly listened to her and when I talked, it was as if the Spirit was talking through me. However, once I got high, she would visit and I would talk all the time telling her what I knew, like I thought I was the teacher and wise man—not let her talk at all. I guess I was just fooling myself, but she would smile and then I would not see her for a month or two. Now, it has been a long time and I miss her medicine. I miss her so much, but I am so far gone. Do you think Sam, I have a chance? Every day I wake up and say in three months I will be clean, but three months pass and I am worse than ever, and my spirit sinks so low that partying, drinking and drugging is the only answer. Sometimes, I sit on my bed smoking the powder and all I can think about are crazy desperate sex, more powder and booze—and this is all that I want or feel I need. And I dream of more free money so I will not have to worry."

Sam said, "I know it is hard to have and then not have. And to feel guilty about your life is one of the most difficult feelings for us humans to accept. But my friend, there is an answer. You just have to find it."

Surprisingly, all the fogginess and confusion which were Jimmy's constant friends suddenly evaporated and for the first time in months, he felt clear headed and hopeful. Then Jimmy looked strangely and said, "I don't know why I am telling you all this, I never talk to strangers."

Sam said, "I am known as 'the smiling fool' by some and 'the messenger' by others, and I am looking for a certain wisdom and power, someone who is not afraid of the unknown. May I ask, what is the name of this woman you talked about?"

He responded with a wistful look on his face, "Oh, Alita. I think she would like you." Sam relaxed with the hearing of the same name the Chief had mentioned to him.

Jimmy then smiled warmly and asked about a ride to his home on a West Coast reservation, and told him if he did not have a place to stay, he could spend the night at his place. Sam suggested they even might see Alita while he was at Jimmy's, of which Jimmy flashed a toothy smile and laughed in a high pitched voice.

They left shortly as Jimmy was suddenly feeling sleepy and tired out. 'The messenger' felt chills go down his back as he wondered if Alita would be unique. He packed his drum and waved goodbye to all his fellow drummers. They wished him good journeys, and as he stepped out of the hall, Vancouver was experiencing an unexpected and rare snowstorm!

Chapter 20
The Reserve

Hugh flakes of snow pierced the sky as he drove to Jimmy's small reserve right next to the ocean. They felt a relaxed and quiet feeling driving slowly and steadily through the slippery snowy roads. Jimmy seemed to gather his second wind, mentioning his Reserve (tribe or nation) was close to signing their Treaty with the provincial and federal governments and that the Chief was intensely involved with the negotiations. He wondered what 'the messenger' had to say about this. Surprisingly he had a lot to say about it and his tone became sober and business like.

Sam began, "It seems to me Treaty is really just a business agreement involving money and land. The heart of it should be self-government, with a focus on human development and solutions to social problems. However, most Native governments believe in the American model of economic prosperity solving everything, including alcoholism, drugs, sex, violence and a plague of other social problems that most reserves have. It is a bit of a shame. The time is ripe for new, innovative and creative Native solutions, but the Native governments just follow the White man's foolish direction in regards to solving their social problems.

The White man is lost in these areas because their solutions revolve around archaic psychological and psychiatric techniques that attempt to cope with, rather than heal human problems. The Native leaders have their heads into making money and not into helping their desperate people. They seem to have no leadership or ideas in these human areas, except to copy White man solutions which have proven time and again to fail and to fail miserably. Money did not solve your social and human problems, Jimmy, nor will it solve your friends' or their kids' problems. What is needed is an enlightened perspective or a 'new way of SEEing'. Chiefs may become recognized and powerful in their political and economic thrusts, but most could not solve their own psychological dilemmas, let alone have one good idea about how to solve their own community's. The greatest asset is not how rich in resources or cash a community is, but how strong and wise the members are.

"Yes, but what you are saying," said an agitated Jimmy, "is that we are hopeless, and mustn't we find our own way?"

'The messenger' stated, "No, you are no more hopeless than almost all of society, and it finds a way to survive and prosper. It is true you must find your own way, but honestly Jimmy, wouldn't it be better if it wasn't only your own way, but a wise way—a way which honestly develops a healthy community. However, what do I know? After all, I am only a White Man."

Jimmy could kind of see Sam's point of view, especially since he sounded a bit like Alita, who often had expressed her frustration with present day psychiatric and psychological approaches. Jimmy had often thought Alita was too strong in her criticism of these doctors as he felt they knew more than her on the topic; after all they were doctors and had gone to university, and they all seemed to agree with each other. Now, after hearing Sam, he was not so sure. Jimmy thought to himself, "Yes, I would like to be a fly on the wall when these two meet."

'The messenger' continued by saying, "Doctors often talk about good stress and bad stress, but if you look at the definition of stress in the dictionary, it is always associated with nervous tension, anxiety and worry leading to trauma. Once I talked to a doctor who believed in outside factors causing stress and he gave the example of congested traffic. I asked him, "Why one person feels stress in this situation and another doesn't? He acknowledged the person's thinking does seem to play a part in the equation, but dismissed my query as it contradicted his existing opinions."

Finally the driving was over; they arrived at Jimmy's gray aluminum siding home on the Reservation. Sam's car slid and spun its tires, but was able to pull into the gravel driveway, which was covered with about two inches of snow. They both laughed like kids as they opened their doors and came into contact with the falling snow and the newly created winter wonderland.

It was a two bedroom mobile home with a foundation. Although it was not more than two years old, it had a tired look, with one or two holes in the walls, beer spills on the carpets, and grime and dirt—especially in the kitchen and bathroom. However, it did have a large modern looking TV with a satellite connection. Jimmy mentioned he loved TV, especially watching wrestling which he and his friends never missed. Jimmy directed Sam to the extra bedroom, which thankfully had clean sheets and was in good repair.

Coffee was put on and then the two sat down in the living room and began a gentle talk. Jimmy mentioned he thought he saw a pipe bundle in Sam's belongings.

Sam said, "Sometime soon, we may have a pipe ceremony if you are so inclined".

Sam could see Jimmy was wondering how a White man becomes a Pipe Carrier, and his answer was simply, "I enjoy educating People in different ways and many Native and non-Native are more receptive to Native teachings from me rather than a Native person. All of my life I have been fascinated by the different ways that lead to the One Life. Each is a path that takes the traveler past different sights and experiences. In the end, however, the destination is still the same. I believe we are all one, Jimmy. Your life, the life of tens of creatures' unseen, living in the rocks, or the highest treetops, is One Life. When we kill or hate others, we kill or hate ourselves. Life is a series of circles within circles, never ending. If a man faithfully walks the spiral to the center, and doesn't fall off, he will eventually find the solution."

Jimmy gave him a curious look. "Is that an answer?"

'The messenger' smiled, "It is the only answer. Apparently you have not found the question yet." They both laughed.

Jimmy said, "Why don't we watch some TV?"

Luckily, the movie, 'A Love Song for Bobby Long' was just beginning. John Travolta played Bobby Long; a shrewd and brilliant professor who was also an alcoholic. While watching the movie, Jimmy stated he had heard and was convinced that alcohol is a disease.

'The messenger' answered, "That is 100% rubbish. All it is; is a bad habit. How could it be a disease? When you were not drinking, the disease was not there. Now that you are drinking it is a convenient way to justify your drinking. Many in the world believe in the disease concept, but that does not make it true."

Jimmy brought up he had heard the disease was simply hibernating when he was not drinking.

Sam replied, "Again, I say, this is nonsense! Every thought is inside you and will come out to play in unpredictable fashions. If you choose to activate an impure or tainted thought, you must pay the penalty for such. I know the urge seems impossible to resist, yet somewhere deep in the recesses of your consciousness, you are aware of what you are doing. One day, Jimmy, you will have an epiphany, and leaving alcohol behind will be one of the easiest things you have ever done. Yet today, it is one of the most difficult—another one of life's puzzles.

Jimmy, once I heard this story about a Lakota who was called the Cat, because a cat lives nine lives. He had a vicious drinking habit and one night he passed out in a snowdrift and a snow blower came along and blew him out of the machine and he survived. Another time while inebriated, a train hit him and he survived. On another cold night, he fell asleep outside in a snowstorm and survived again. Then, one day, he met an astute psychologist who explained to him it was his confused personal thoughts which were at the origin of the problem. He heard 'something special' and he never drank a drop of alcohol again. Now, he teaches his People about the curing Power he experienced from this epiphany (insight)."

"Well, that is good medicine about alcohol, but the white powder is something totally different," retorted Jimmy, "And my son is hopelessly caught in that world."

"You must first understand your son's cocaine addiction is a symptom of a much more deep-set problem. The real source of his crisis is what I call the *'negative effects of the boomerang'*. Negative thoughts react like a boomerang turning into ugly feelings. Contrarily positive thoughts boomerang back into positive feelings. For example, after an ex-cocaine addict experienced the healing Power, I asked her how she had 'kicked the habit'. She mentioned she had been on cocaine for twenty-five years and then profoundly said when she found a better high than cocaine that is where she went.

You cannot possibly think your way through this; it is not an intellectual exercise. You have to look beyond your son's symptoms for a spiritual answer. Your son is the only one who can uncover the answer to his problem. No outside solution exists; no amount of will power or mental force will solve his problem. He must look within and see Truth, and then all solutions are possible.

And, Jimmy, who knows, maybe together we can uncover some positive feelings to help us against our own bad habits and urges. We can at least be thankful we have met each other."

Jimmy responded, "My urges overpower me, why am I powerless against them. Tell me about the darker side of life?"

Sam sighed compassionately. "A negative urge is a dark thought pattern which has been repeated countless times, usually over an extended period of time. After awhile we succumb to its allure. Compare it to the electricity of a seductive, voluptuous woman who drives a lonely man crazy. In fact after a lifetime of repeating these dark thought patterns, they appear to have an unlimited power. They create an illusion they are more powerful than you are, or even worse that the source of the urge is outside of yourself.

Of course each time the urge is expressed, psychological imbalances such as fear, stress, disgust, and guilt are experienced. Sometimes, these, over time, can lead to long-term chemical imbalances, addictions and severe psychosis patterns.

Trace back the puzzle in the above two paragraphs, and Jimmy, you may come to realize the *first cause* of long-term chemical imbalances, addictions and severe psychosis patterns is drawn from *thought*."

Jimmy quickly retorted. "But why are they so powerful, if urges are only a thought pattern?"

"Great question," answered Sam. "All thought (even ego thought) has the power of God behind it. It is God which gives life to all thought, so why should it not be powerful. That is why we have free will and consciousness. Choose wisely and your life and feelings will be successful. Choose unwisely and the pattern of life (or your destiny) will head in the direction of 'temporary doom'.

Jimmy smiled, agreed and suggested they go to sleep, for tomorrow promised to be an adventure.

Chapter 21
The Next Day

Angel *is used to translate the Hebrew word of the Old Testament pronounced mal-awk, and the Greek word of the New Testament pronounced ang-el-os. Both original words mean* **messenger.**

Early the next morning, Sam made coffee, toast, bacon and eggs which had been stored in his car. Jimmy groggily woke up after answering a telephone call; he gladly ate some of the breakfast, and then said, "Tell me a bit of your story, Sam."

"Well, it is a typical story of the youth of the late 60's and early 70's. After graduating from University, I entered the workforce as an investment analyst with a very large company; however, I quickly became disillusioned. Politics and bureaucracy within the company were emphasized, rather than effectiveness and reason. I got into some serious drinking, partying and then simply quit my job, even though it was prestigious and high paying. I traveled to Europe for over a year and began to experience a concept called *the illusion of time*. After about 6 or 7 months of traveling, forgetting about time, and letting my mind flow with whatever life brought, I did not even know what month it was. I decided to buy a Herald

Tribune, which was the American paper in Europe, and to my surprise I had miss-guessed the date by several months. And then to my disbelief, the newspaper headlines were exactly the same as when I had last looked except the sports season had changed. Somehow I began to understand the absurdity and futility of the world. There had to be more than this and thus, I began my spiritual search.

I traveled back to Canada and moved to Vancouver and began my pursuit of becoming a hippy, drugs and spirituality. I tried all the major consciousness raising trips (what we called them back in the 70's). Hari Krishna was my first exposure and I progressed through many others, especially if it was free or cheap. I listened to gurus (so called enlightened beings) and even had a stint with the psychic reality of Tarot cards. The latter was interesting especially when all types of people started to phone for my advice with the Tarot cards. People will obviously listen to anyone especially if it has the illusion of being part of the occult."

"What did you learn from Hari Krishna, it looks so weird?" asked Jimmy.

"Well, I never really became a Hari Krishna disciple, but I took a few positives from it. First, I loved their discussions and delicious free food of vegetables and dairy products. I remember talking to a disgruntled disciple. He was getting up about four in the morning, working from morning to night and, in his opinion, not gaining any spiritual insights. He mentioned Hari Krishna teaches that life is a battle waged inside us. I could not understand what he meant, and he said he did not know either but he heard it was supposed to be something quite amazing when we experienced it. Well, I left the ashram (community formed primarily for spiritual upliftment of its members, often headed by a religious leader or mystic) and never went back again but his idea of a 'battle within me' continued to fascinate my mind. Now, I understand what he is talking about, and while I cannot tell you what it means except to call it the battle between ego and truth, with ego winning much of the time."

Jimmy was an expert on having troubled thoughts, so he understood the battle but the wisdom of how to escape these thoughts were beyond him. He smiled and asked, "What was life like as a hippy?"

"Actually, it was a lot better than most people today gave it credit for. For instance, I went to the most historical pop festival the world has ever experienced. It was called Woodstock and over 500,000 youth were in attendance, just outside of New York City. It was one of the most mystical experiences the world has ever experienced. I know it changed my life forever. It was peaceful; in my opinion, the present state of the world's youth could never experience this Power peacefully. In fact, today the world does not even believe in Peace; in those days, the hippies all believed in Peace as a destined reality. The festival was situated in a farmer's field a ways from New York City. It was totally surrounded with fences and they pre-sold about 80,000 tickets and left about 10,000 tickets to be sold at the gate. Well, over 75,000 youth from all over USA and Canada showed up for the 10,000 tickets, so the overflowing crowd standing in line pushed the fences down. The promoters decided to make it a free concert rather than 'go for the money', and this made the festival special. Additionally, it was a hot day in New York City and all the hippies and youth heard there was a free concert a few miles away and they poured into the festival. Most of the best bands in the world played there, from Jimi Hendrix, Janis Joplin, Joan Baez and so on. Bands that were unheard of became famous overnight like Santana. But it was not the bands which were the stars of the festival; it was the *crowd* and their camaraderie. They screamed in ecstasy and experienced the music in Oneness. You could not get the bands to leave the revolving stage, because they knew they would never play before such an awesome audience like this ever again—it was impossible because it was a *'once in a lifetime event'*.

Unfortunately as the years rolled on, most hippies became plastic or superficial as hippism became fashionable. Then, it revolved mostly around sex, drugs and pretending to be 'cool'. This was not the case in the beginning. In the late 60's, the world's perspective had gotten so narrow in its conservative attitudes; creativity and inspiration were stifled. The world had to change and the cultural youth of yesterday understood this better than the adults. The hippies separated from society, and it appears this was wrong as you can not make permanent change without integrating within society. However, the world was never the same and I am proud to say, I would not be where I am today without these mind lifting experiences."

"When you were traveling and living as a hippy, did you use drugs?" asked Jimmy.

"Oh yes, that was one of my main objectives when I went to live in Vancouver. I tried just about everything, although I kept away from hard drugs. Marijuana, hash and a small sampling of LSD (acid) were my main staples. Now I do not use these, but at the time, in my opinion it was a required part of my personal and spiritual development. You see, to me life was so staid and restricted in its thinking; I just had to explore beyond the antiquated, status quo world's thinking. And of course, now the world would agree it was 'stupid' in most of those antiquated ideas, but times were different then, and unfortunately, I would suggest the world is even more 'chaotic and speedy' now in comparison to those times.

"Aren't drugs destructive?" asked Jimmy.

"Some. Hard drugs are very destructive. In fact I would keep as far away from cocaine, heroin, crystal meth, etc. As you personally know, they conquer your will power. An addicted mind is 'out of balance'; life becomes weird and insane. Your desires become like a dog chasing its own tail. You see, soft drugs are not addictive. So for me they were pleasurable and useful allies. I was too regimented and they opened my horizons. Yet at another point, my mind does not require their stimuli. Once in a while I will have a beer or a joint, but these are extremely rare occasions. Alcohol is a legal downer and I know many use it today to relieve stress, and in extreme moderation, it is effective for such. However, many people drink far too much, and its destructive powers are underestimated by today's youth and adults. Do you know what is comforting, Jimmy? Since I have tried both alcohol and drugs, I am an expert because I talk from personal experience. 90% of the world talks from what they hear from the politicians or 'experts????' Now, which is more scientific—what I have experienced or what they believe."

Jimmy stated, "I cannot seem to run away from my vices, especially alcohol and cocaine. They chase me everywhere I go. Messenger, can you help me?"

"Jimmy, bad thoughts are like tiny holes in a glass. Pretty soon they will make you dry and empty. Very soon now you must decide whether your glass will be eternally empty with anger, despair and resentment or full with love and peace. Which will it be?

It is the empty chamber that makes a drum beautiful. Without emptiness there would be no music. Emptiness is also what makes love possible. Jimmy, all wise sages talk about the quieting of the personal mind to bring us back into harmony with the silence of the Great Spirit."

Jimmy decided to change the topic as he was feeling uncomfortable with the conversation, so he asked another question. "Well, you were a hippy in pursuit of the Spirit, then what happened?"

"I was earnestly involved in finding a spiritual answer to life and, as luck would have it, I met 'One Who Knows'; he guided me to look inside myself. He always stated what I was looking for would be found 'within' rather than in the worship and glorification of him. I listened to this man and could not figure out what he was talking about. I intuitively knew he was enlightened when I heard him talk at an event called the Gathering of the Ways, but my life did not change. Then, one day about one month after several meetings with 'One Who Knows', I had a simple but life changing experience. I was walking around a lake when, all of a sudden, my mind became perfectly Quiet. All my personal thoughts stopped for about fifteen to twenty minutes; there I was listening to Nature without any thinking. It was so serene; I will never forget the peacefulness and wonderment of those moments. I was connected to all of Nature; I was walking in astonishment at how beautiful and insightful life is. I could hear the birds in a way that I describe as crystal clear. I was not 'a product of my thinking' for the first time in my life— I was Me and it was Still. Therefore, Jimmy, I always tell people they will find the answer in the silence, yet I know they do not understand, because I do not really understand that myself. Crazy, isn't it, I experienced something so profound that I cannot explain it and many times disbelieve it myself—what a mystery life is!

My life totally changed after that and over time, I became happy and content. I may have caught a glimpse of the iceberg, but unfortunately, I cannot describe or guide you to the iceberg. That is why I am called 'the messenger'.

After that I started to try to help People, and this was very difficult for me, as I am not very good at it. However, over time life took me to the Native People and while I must say they are challenging, I have enjoyed my glimpse into your worlds.

I was guided by the Great Spirit to the mountains of British Columbia and it was there I randomly met a Native woman. We talked about the beauty of the mountains, and we both saw how the White man's greed was destroying many of the clear cut trees on the mountains; I felt Mother Earth's pain. Obviously, most businessmen do not understand that the Earth is alive. This experience totally disgusted me but my compassion grew.

It was not long before I began working and learning about the intricate nature of the Natives and their communities. Do you know what the biggest problem, in my mind, is with Native communities? It is not poverty, or drugs and drinking, or sexual perversions or violence. It is *gossip*; it destroys so many people in the community and it destroys much of the hope that a community needs to fulfill its destiny and potential.

You are a difficult people to understand, but when it comes to intelligence, laughter and enjoyment, the Native People are at the top of the list. The understanding of the Spiritual nature of a human being is intrinsic to most Natives, but their understanding of how to solve their psychological problems is extremely low. I have searched for someone who knows how to listen to the hum above what the general consensus says, and have not found the one Native that I am looking for up to now.

Speaking of that, is there any opportunity to meet this lady called Alita? I would like to talk with her?"

Jimmy said, "It is interesting you should ask, for her phone call woke me up this morning, she suggested we have lunch today at my place, so you are in luck."

Sam wondered if this time, destiny was going to be on his side. He was beginning to wonder if there was ever going to be an Indian who wanted his message.

Chapter 22
Alita's Visit

Sam drove into the neighboring town, as the snowy roads had been plowed, and purchased some groceries for Jimmy's empty cupboards; a Bar B Que chicken, some healthy salads and a delicious mocha chocolate cake. He returned to Jimmy's home and they began to set the table for lunch. Sure enough, around noon a car rolled into the driveway and Alita strolled up to the door, opened it and said, "Anyone home." A big smile showed on her face as she hugged Jimmy and was introduced to Sam.

Alita looked coyly at the new stranger in Jimmy's house. He did not have the look of the others she had met at Jimmy's. She could sense some latent Power in the man, and she could not help but admit he was kind of cute for 'an ugly white man'. Some strange feeling began gnawing at her. A sense of her recent dream gently awoke in her. She asked Jimmy, "Who is your friend?"

"He is called Sam 'the messenger' and he knows of the Indian ways. He feels he is aware of something the Indians need to know. He says it is so obvious. That is why we cannot see it."

"Oh," said Alita, intrigued by such an elaborate introduction.

Jimmy continued by saying, "He has heard something from 'Someone Who Knows' and this is part of his message. I hope you can understand him Alita because I do not really know what he saying, but my feelings tell me he is speaking the truth. He is a man of Power, to be sure, and he does know our ways. He even practices sacred ceremonies and his drum sings to our hearts."

Alita was curious about this 'Someone Who Knows'. "Do you mean this person is enlightened?"

"Yes," said Sam. "He talks about how we live in a world governed by thought. He points to the Spiritual Source as the answer to all problems here on earth; his understanding includes how formlessness creates form. Therefore, he sees and knows not only this material world but its connection to the world of Spirit. If you ever have the honor to be in the presence of such a man or woman, my advice is relax and enjoy the experience with a quiet mind. Then, maybe something of a 'more profound reality' or Truth might creep into your consciousness, and you will forever be changed.

This has been my experience with him. I wish I could hear more than I have, but that seems to be controlled by the Great Spirit, and when I am ready, I am sure I will. But today, I come to you as 'a messenger' who can describe some of the benefits of listening to this man's impersonal wisdom; a wisdom which includes the connection between the spiritual and psychological worlds.

"Interesting, could you tell me what you see or heard was his experience of enlightenment?" asked Alita.

"He mentioned he did see the folly of his own thinking; specifically that he was fearful and insecure and realized, in one instance, *fear or insecurity is only a thought*. This guided him to his enlightening experience. A few days later after his first insight, he metaphorically left this world while walking through a tunnel of dazzling white light and when he came back, life as he knew it had totally changed. He had no university education or spiritual training, yet he knew all about God, Universal Mind and the Spirit World. Obviously, his experience had nothing to do with gender, age or past experiences. He felt he just happened to 'be lucky'. This is all I can say, at this time."

"Did he direct you towards only being positive, or always living in positive energy?" asked Jimmy.

"Not really, anyway not as the world seems to preach it in today's archaic theories and man-interpreted religions. However, he does emphasize the benefits of positive feelings and living in the Now. I am not really knowledgeable in many of these questions, but if we talk about them, maybe we will uncover a wiser dimension; one which alleviates so much of the suffering of your People, if that is your desire."

A tear came to Alita's eye as this was her biggest dream of life. Some strange feelings eased their way into her heart. Some vague memories of her vision in the cave resurfaced.

The messenger continued, "Once, while up on a mountain with this wise teacher, I saw something extraordinary—special to me anyway. I experienced the 'boomerang effect' of my actions and thoughts, for instance if we exhibit an aggressive nature, this must and does instantly boomerang back into us. Vice versa, when one spreads gentleness and understanding, this will produce a gentle and wise life. This 'boomerang' changed my perspective on life.

Alita tilted her head and decided to further explore Sam's mind by asking, "What is your visual image of the Great Spirit or God?"

The Metaphor

"Well, I can try Alita but since it is impossible to describe, obviously I will fail.

Imagine inside you is a sacred tree, which unveils all the mysteries of the universe. This sacred tree is not outside of yourself, it is integrated, interconnected and lives because of your consciousness of it. It is always alive and full of fruit. However, sometimes we put a blanket over the tree, and because of this blanket we cannot see or feel the tree—it seems we appear to lose *our connection* to what we truly are.

In this metaphor, tainted thoughts lead us to produce a blanket of insecure and fearful feelings about life, the world, and our selves. This produces feelings of anxiety, loneliness, guilt, anger and so on. Each impure thought weaves the blanket and makes it appear thicker, stronger and more real. Contrarily, positive thought leads to feelings which lifts the blanket and uncovers the sacred tree.

The source of this tree is the Great Spirit, which is connected to YOU. You and the Great Spirit are ONE and this sacred tree is the point of common ONENESS."

Alita was enjoying this conversation, and after lunch she suggested that 'the messenger' attend a sweat with her. She further suggested, since the sweat was in several hours, they could go for a walk near the ocean. He smiled and said to Jimmy, "I guess we are off. See you later."

Jimmy laughed, seeing something in Alita he had never seen before. "After all," he smiled to himself, "she is a woman," and this is something Jimmy knew about.

Chapter 23
The Walk Together

Alita and Sam cozily walked to the ocean. The conversation drifted in many different directions. Alita was quickly warming up to this man; she was intrigued with his gentle nature and wise mind. She recognized she could learn much from this man, even about her own insecurities and spiritual questions, while sharing some of her precious feelings and sacred knowledge.

Sam nonchalantly began to talk about his early pursuits into seeing the oneness of spiritual and material life via mathematics. "I started to hypothesize that the answer to the conundrum might lie in the fact we live in a three-dimensional (3-D) material world. Mathematically, we use length, width and height for calculations in our three-dimensional world. In truth, length is the same as width or height, yet we use three different words. I came to understand our minds require these three principles to illustrate the physical Oneness.

Let me give you a personal example to demonstrate this. In University, I studied Calculus (Calculus is the study of change, in the same way that geometry is the study of shape, and algebra is the study of operations and their application to solving equations[4]). I was an expert with the numbers and formulas of algebra, but absolutely hopeless at visualizing the geometric concepts of calculus. I would draw out a 3-D cube on paper and it would not become form. I COULD NOT GET IT! I COULD NOT SEE IT! My frustrated mind puzzled and puzzled over the question of how does a 2-D piece of paper describe 3-D? Then, one day, as my mind relaxed, I SAW it, I saw 3-D rather than 2-D, and Calculus instantly became more alive for me.

That is the same with length, width and height. Once a person sees one, the requirement of all three becomes obvious. Perhaps, one day our world will talk about the three spiritual principles on formlessness creating form, in the same way I have described length, width and height."

He casually continued to talk about himself. To Alita's surprise, he still considered himself an athlete. Alita mentioned she often was confused with the way the world approaches sport, especially the intense competitive and 'win at all costs' mentality it seemed to engender. "Sam, how do you see this?"

Sam began, "Well, competition has always been my pleasure and my demon. I definitely have seen competition as a negative desire in myself and in others. On the other hand, I love the exercise, pleasure and, above all, the 'magic' in playing sport.

I once read about Jack Nicklaus, the world's greatest golfer before Tiger Woods, as he described being 'in the zone' or a 'state of meditation'. He described it something like this—in a way, he was in a dream state—almost as a third person, he was watching himself swinging and hitting the ball *perfectly*. He was there physically, yet he was inside himself observing the magic happen. It was spiritual because he was connected to the Universal Energy of life. He said it was a *state of mind*, though he could never create it on command although he could access it, and then the wonder and perfection of golf and life revealed itself."

"Could you give me a First Nation example rather than sport analogy?" asked Alita to gain further insight on the subject.

"OK. In a recent sweat, I talked about Fools Crow, a very wise medicine man, and student of Black Elk. Fools Crow said, 'But as I have used hollow bones for curing, I have decided that is better to think of medicine people as little hollow bones. All medicine persons are hollow bones that Wakan-Tanka, Tunkashila, and the Helpers (Sioux words for God or Great Spirit) work through. As I emptied myself out, I could feel more power coming into me, and it was wonderful. That is how I become *a little hollow tube'*.

Black Elk, whom I consider to be the wisest of medicine men stated, 'I cured with the Power that came through me. Of course it was not I who cured. It was the power from the outer world, and the visions and ceremonies had only made me like a hole through which the power could come to the two-leggeds. If I thought that I was doing it myself, the hole would close up and no power could come through. Then everything I could do would be foolish'.

Immediately after finishing my talk in the sweat, a young lady mentioned that while men often talk about humbleness, it is important for women to talk about the greatness of who they are. I found this to be quite profound because in the 'state of meditation', we experience the power of the Universe.

Does that answer your question, Alita about competition and awareness?"

Alita nodded, and then asked, "If competition can become a negative state of mind, how do you see the world? Is it in a state of crisis? And why doesn't the world change for the good more often?"

Sam quickly answered, "The fact that change does happen is the key. That is hope. We must be hopeful; or else we will lose— guaranteed.

Yes, it is an interesting time, with so much of the world obsessed with material possessions, with greed rampant and the ego controlling much of the world. I heard an interesting statistic. In the last 100 years, man has killed over 1.7 billion of his fellow men. With the continued advances in technological weaponry, we, with our lack of decency, are destroying the world."

"Is that what you see?" asked Alita.

"It is one of the possibilities if the world's consciousness does not rise. The Mayan Prophecy of Mexico suggests we are in the fifth or sixth of seven rebirths of the world, but I honestly do not know anything about Mayan beliefs.

Yes, it is one of the possibilities. Another is the world's viewpoint will change in a positive direction—then all of life will change. Perhaps the Americans will elect a more enlightened President, or perhaps a wise man will inspire the world into hope and change. The cumulative effect of human beings contributing, each in their small way, will produce the grassroots result we dream of.

Let me try to give two historical examples where, in my opinion, a culture &/or the world evolved i.e. firstly, the Viking Age and secondly, the Greek 'Age of Reason'.

The Vikings were those people who lived in Scandinavia and the North Atlantic settlements between 793 and 1066 and they, with their gods, had what is described as Pagan beliefs which are quite similar to the Native beliefs. Like the Greeks and the Romans before them, the Vikings worshipped many gods: Odin was the chief of the gods and the ruler of the universe, Thor the god of thunder and war, Freyja the goddess of beauty and love, while another called Loki was half god, half fire spirit and full of mischief like the Coyote stories of the Native People. The Vikings believed the many different gods lived in a place called Asgard, which is similar to how Native Elders describe the 'Other Side'.

In my studies of pre and post Judaic Christian times, much of the world's religion was Paganism in various forms. For example, even long after Christ was born, the Norse mythology of the Viking's had similar beliefs to the Christians. The Christians worship God and the Son of God as the same thing, as depicted by their holy Trinity of the Father, Son and Holy Spirit. The Natives connect Mother Earth and Father Sky. In my opinion, ancient Norse Spirituality is as noble and earth-healing as those of the Far East or Native America.

I just happen to have a Norse poem in my pocket. Let me read it to you. (Sam read the following): *Orlog* is the essential and unchanging laws of the universe that both drive and limit the events presently taking place in our world.

Orlog (The Norns' Chant)

In the midst of darkness, light;
In the midst of death, life;
In the midst of chaos, order.
In the midst of order, chaos;
In the midst of life, death;
In the midst of light, darkness.
Thus has it ever been,
Thus is it now, and
Thus shall it always be.

Alita loved the way Sam read these sacred words.

He continued with his Viking story, "It was during these 300 years that these northern people had the largest impact on other Europeans, through trade and raids. Raiding was actually a part time occupation, practiced by a small percentage of the population. Few Vikings were professional soldiers, although like all men in this era, they were familiar with the use of weapons.

They were farmers first and needed to take care of the farm chores most of the year. They were entrepreneurs; business men who saw raiding as a means of acquiring capital that could be invested in a ship, farm, or business. Raiding was thought to be desirable for a young man, but a more mature man was expected to settle down on the farm and raise a family.

Now, as I suggested, the Vikings were much like the Native Indians in their beliefs and rituals. They also were extremely warlike conquering other tribes of various countries, from the North, South, East and West of Denmark. Their technology of boats and ships were superior to the rest of the existing world. Their defense of their headquarters at Roskilde, about ½ hour car ride outside of Kobenhavn or Copenhagen is legendary. The only way by water to approach Roskilde was via the Danish Fjords (fjord is a long, narrow bay with steep sides, created in a valley) which were entered to by the body of water between Sweden and Denmark. The Vikings simply went to the entrance of the Fjords and sunk three large ships with huge rocks, one on top of the other, to totally block the entrance from war ships of other tribes. Huge parts of these three ships are shown in the Viking Museum at Roskilde, having being preserved by the mud over the countless years.

And not only were they fearless on the seas and lands with the assistance of their gods and spirits, their appetite knew no boundaries. Their boats were so amazing they even traveled from Denmark to below Iceland through the most dangerous icebergs and cold waters all the way down to Canada, an amazing feat when you see how small their ships were. They also went the other way to Russia, down to Africa as well as continually warring with England and Ireland. Because of their advancement of shipbuilding technology, their warlike nature was killing an awful lot of people, much as is happening now.

Interestingly, the Vikings weren't conquered. The Viking age ended when the raids stopped because the rival tribes of England, Ireland etc. grew to be equal in their fighting abilities. Because there were fewer and fewer raids, to the rest of Europe they became not Vikings, but Danes, Swedes, Norwegians, Icelanders and Greenlanders. Now, they are among the most peace loving people of our world and demonstrate, in my opinion, how a culture can change.

Now to my second example which indicates world change. The Greek 'Age of Reason' was the beginning of modern civilization as we know it. It influenced the development of modern religion via the Jewish People and then the development of Christian and Muslim religions. At its geographical peak, Greek civilization spread from Greece to Egypt and to the Hindu Kush mountains in Pakistan. Ancient Greece is considered by most historians to be the foundational culture of Western Civilization. In their golden time, one or more enlightened prophets and their students emerged. The one I am particularly fond of is Socrates who is known as the 'Father of Ethics'. Socrates wrote nothing, so we are dependent upon his students or disciples for any detailed knowledge of his pursuit for truth. Socrates stressed the ideal life was spent in search of the Good and that Truth lies beneath the shadows of existence. He died in 399 BC. His most famous student/disciple was Plato whom the world probably worships to a greater extent, but it is my opinion that, while Plato was highly evolved, he was not enlightened as Socrates was. Plato's famous student was Aristotle who attempted to record the entirety of 'knowledge' of his time, even delving into philosophical thought on topics like Infinity, The Spirit of Music, The Immateriality of Mind, and God. Both Plato and Aristotle are famous for their schools.

So we see when, in past times, the world was in a state of crisis, much as we are now, there emerged a more profound perspective of life, which either featured fewer killings and an avoidance of massive destructions, or the passing of greater wisdom to the masses. I realize many more humans than necessary have died. This is unfortunate! But our world did evolve in spite of the continued injustices perpetrated by the political and religious leaders of the time.

For example, after reading the book, Roots by Arthur Hailey, who stated, his wise and intelligent great-great-great grandfather, Kunta Kinte, from Gambia, West Africa was *greedily captured* by slave traders and put on a slave ship to America in the 1750's, his own father had become a professor at an University and had evolved into living a rich and successful life as a parent and human being.

It is the same now. The world is amuck with greed; it controls the minds of mankind and of their leaders. As some of the masses start to honestly want a spiritual change—from the archaic and backward thinking where greed, selfishness and lack of hope for positive change prevails—there exists the possibility of a shift in world consciousness from what the world has experienced thus far. The world could become a better, more creative place; and many negative aspects could disappear forever. Perhaps this time, the shift will be more spiritual and profound in nature. This is how I see a possible outcome or destiny to the present world's situation. Of course, this vision is inclusive of the current ecological challenges.

Alita was fascinated with this talk, as she had never imagined a possible connection between her People and the Vikings, realizing that they possessed similar spiritual beliefs, a sense of honor and a fearlessness to live within the limits provided by Mother Nature; or a connection to advanced Greek thinking and even African American history. She liked this! It made sense to her! She was becoming fascinated with this man. He was not only spiritual; he was knowledgeable, insightful and she realized she hadn't been in touch with one such as him before.

"This is good," she whispered to herself.

Chapter 24
The Sweat

She said to Sam with tenderness, "It is time for the sweat." They held hands as they walked back to where the sweat was being held. However, upon coming to the possibility of meeting others, their hands separated. Alita introduced Sam to a few of the others at the sweat, but before she knew it, he was shaking hands with everyone, introducing himself.

She chuckled to herself. "Obviously, he can take care of himself."

Before the sweat began, with the rocks heating up in the raging fire, Sam noticed a young 'up tight' non-Native woman with a serious expression on her face. Sam could sense that there was an experience awaiting her in the sacred ceremony. He walked up to her. Upon finding it was to be her first sweat, Sam warmly gave her some advice. "Relax and enjoy. Don't try to figure it out. The first round will relax your body. The more relaxed you are, the better it will be for you. I have heard Black Fox is a wise and gentle teacher." Sam saw her relax right on the spot and a warm bond of trust was established between the two of them.

The first three rounds of the sweat were powerful and uplifting. Black Fox gave some advice in the woman's round to the young lady. "Many people think there are two powers that we live by, but this is incorrect. There is only one power."

In the fourth round, anyone who wished to talk was encouraged to do so. When there was a pause between the speakers, Sam began. "To the Grandfathers and Grandmothers, my Indian name is Kuc-kun-niwi or 'Little Wolf'. Early this morning, I drove by a church. It had about a 1000 cars parked outside, and I wondered what had brought so many people out on a Saturday afternoon. I looked at the church sign and it was a three day symposium on fear. Obviously, fear is a big topic out in the world. And do you know what causes fear? It is the little mind! This little mind constantly thinks about 'what isn't' rather than 'what is'. Our little mind thinks and causes all our self-made problems in this world and its amigo is fear and insecurity—thus, as Black Fox would say, leading us down the black road. The Big Mind or Great Spirit is the world of 'is-ness' and its amigo is love and understanding—thus, we experience the red road.

It is as Black Fox says, 'There is only one power, not two'. There is only One Mind, even though many believe there are two.

Now, I would like to talk about a simple experience I had recently. For the past two years my right arm was sore throughout, especially in the shoulder region. Pain was always rampant in my bicep and I could not move it easily. I became more and more fearful whenever I used it. Then, a few days ago, I suffered a severe pain in the shoulder, and several experts suggested I was finished playing all sports which involved my shoulder and arm. However, my kind doctor arranged for me to see a specialist. Several hours later his office phoned *in a panic* as the specialist was worried about the possibility of my bicep being ruptured. The next day I was waiting, as instructed, in the emergency section of the hospital and the specialist came out. He said miraculous words—it was like poetry to my heart. He said the bicep tendon had severed, but *there was nothing to worry about* because the rest of my body would naturally compensate for it. And he said, 'You probably will notice less pain in your arm. Give it a bit of a rest and then go for it, you can play sports, everything. Don't hold back'. Immediately I felt looseness in my shoulder and felt an ability I had not felt for over two years. But there was a bigger miracle. It was the disappearance of the fear. The fear had started as a tiny thought and it had grown into a huge block, like an enormous block of ice and it melted immediately upon hearing the specialist's words. The baggage of fear was gone and I felt a release that was like a 1000 pounds off my shoulders. I was free."

And Sam continued, "And you know, this fear was all in my...." and Alita could feel everyone in the sweat say to themselves.... 'in your head'. Sam concluded by saying, "This may sound like a small thing but to me, it was a very big thing. *All my relations* (a phrase many Aboriginal people use to indicate the closing of their talk. One of its meanings is—We are *all* related. We should *all* get along)."

Then the young non-Native lady began crying, as if she was connected to Sam's story. She was full of sadness, crying over a difficulty about a family matter, and Grey Wolf stated, "Let it out, let it out. It is a good thing to cry while you are praying." And she did, and was guided through a mystical healing by Black Fox and Grey Wolf.

After the sweat, Sam talked to Alita. "I felt the change in that young lady. She walked into the sweat as a dead but powerful woman, and awoke with aliveness about her life. I saw it in her eyes. She transformed from the dead to life. If what Black Fox said is true, then it makes sense that one of our roles in life is to *get rid of the fear in our self*—to get past the baggage. That is a simple role, and not complicated. And to get rid of this fear, Grey Wolf stated it was a good thing to 'cry while you are praying'.

Alita was finding herself becoming sexually attracted to Sam. He had a charm, which was melting her heart. He was secure and brave, as compared to most men she had met. She gave him her most alluring smile, expecting an immediate response from his manhood, but to her surprise, he ignored it.

Then surprising her again, he turned and walked over to the neighboring house next door and began talking to a man with a blackened (rubbed on removable paint) face. He returned and said to Alita, "See you later, I am going drumming at the Longhouse, I have been invited."

Alita was a little shocked. Not only had her sexual thrust been dismissed, he was off on an adventure that did not include her.

This greatly disturbed and frustrated Alita and she began to have many thoughts like, "He just does not seem to be interested in me as a woman, maybe he only sees me just as a spiritual mate or a student. Is he oblivious to my feelings?"

Chapter 25
The Journey

"Change your thoughts and you change your world."
...*Norman Vincent Peale*

The next morning, Alita's restless mind was unable to get Sam out of her head. Exasperated, she finally gave up and phoned him; she asked if he would be interested in getting together after lunch.

He said, "Sure, let's meet at the beach at 1:00, could you bring some coffee," and she gladly agreed, relieved to be seeing him again.

When one o'clock rolled around, they met at their secret little beach spot. He was smiling as usual, and Alita gave him a genuine smile in return. After a few minutes of enjoying the scenery, he began talking about going to Mexico for a week's holiday about one and a half hours north of Puerto Vallarta. He said he needed a rest and some sun. "I am going to book the hotel in the town of Rincon de Guayabitos because of its local Mexican feeling, two mile beach and its location near to the local Indians, the Huichols. The Huichols are descendants of the Aztecs and one of the last indigenous peoples of Mexico; they live in scattered kinship ranchos (settlements) in the Sierre Madre Mountains not too far from the town. I have never met them but I am curious because they are known to be descendents of the 'Wolf-People', are shamanic in nature, and have maintained their traditions, customs, art and language more strongly than any of the other Indian groups of Mexico. In fact I have done some research on the Internet and found some very interesting info? Do you want to hear about it?"

Alita was struggling with her composure because Sam was leaving her, but she maintained a brave face and said, "Love to."

"My research described them as the last tribe in North America living similarly to pre-Columbia times, in part due to the remoteness of their villages. The Huichol ancestry can be traced back approximately 3,500 years to the Aztecs, by way of the Olmec from south-central Mexico and the Hopi Indians from Arizona. Of course they are struggling to keep their culture and religion alive. Many sell their art to keep from being overtaken by the modern world, though some work in coal mines and at other jobs, in order to feed their families.

'Huichol' (pronounced Wettchol) means doctor or healer, a name they fully deserve as about one-fourth of the men are shamans. They consider themselves the guardians of the earth, and their main Gods are based on fire, wind, water and sun. In order to become a shaman, the Huichol take a pilgrimage to their sacred land for five years in a row. It is here that they gather their peyote (the Divine Cactus has a history of ritual religious and medicinal use among the indigenous) and use it to commune with the Universal forces; it is through these sacred rituals the shamans have visions, which are then ultimately made into art pieces such as yarn paintings, which signify sacred representations of God, of themselves, of Nature—which are all One thing. The Peyote mandalas symbolize the entrance to the spiritual world. Often there is a cleansing ceremony lead by a 'Marakame' (He who knows).

In their mythology, the Huichol evolved from wolves, with shamans claiming the power to transform themselves into spirited wolves. As carrier of the spirits, the wolf is honored in all peyote ceremonies. Rituals generally involve singing, weeping and contact with ancestor spirits.

In the Huichol belief system, humans are like the corn, one in the same because both carry the seed for the future and both require the intervention of the deities to grow and flourish. As I read on the internet, 'Just like people take their babies to the church to be anointed with holy water, we take the souls of our baby corn plants to our gods and goddesses to receive their blessings'.

Anyway, Alita that gives you a nice flavor of it. I just talked to a pipe carrier from El Salvador and he gave me the Indian name for a sweat or purification. It is pronounced 'Te Maz Cal' and I am curious if they have the same type of sweats there, as he said sweat lodges are all the way down from Mexico to South America."

"*Gee, Alita, I just had a thought.* Why don't you come and join me, I am booking the all-inclusive flight, hotel and food this afternoon and we could have a blast together. What do you say?"

Alita was caught flat-footed or flabbergasted, and just stood there with her mouth wide-open. She then smiled and after hearing the cost involved, enthusiastically said, "I am going, let's book it!"

Immediately, the intense feeling of her dream in the cave resurfaced. "Maybe, I will discover the answer to 'So much suffering in her People and she was powerless to help'," she whispered hopefully to herself.

"And maybe, something else."

Chapter 26
Mexico Revisited

Alita was thrilled. She was with Sam and returning to the exotic land of sunny Mexico. She remembered the Mexicans from her previous trip to Cancún. They were like 'wolves in sheep's clothing'. The Spanish influence in their lives was obvious, but inherently they were Mexican Indians.

In the airplane she comfortably settled in beside Sam and began watching a movie called August Rush which had as its central theme, 'The music is all around us, all you have to do is hear it'. She realized there are many worlds out there. "I only have to live mine. I must find my own voice, not someone else's."

Alita turned to Sam and asked, "What did you mean, when you stated 'mental sickness' is the same as a 'computer virus'?"

"Well, a computer virus is some 'pain in the ass' code, which infects the computer and makes it act 'kind of crazy'. For instance, one virus I had would reroute my internet to another website, totally unrelated to what I wanted. In effect, my internet became useless and remained so until a technician removed the virus. The computer was normal after that.

It is the same with 'mental illnesses'. A normal person infects his computer (brain) with some kind of addictive behavior; for example extreme anger, frustration, sexual desires, or depression. This thought pattern becomes habitual and takes over the normal thinking of a human being, making him appear to be 'mentally ill'. Some doctors notice the chemical imbalances, which are due to 'out of balance' behavior, but this is actually the same as noticing that the internet is being rerouted.

The chemical imbalances will disappear, if and when, the 'so called sick person' gets rid of his 'virus'—in this case, addictive thinking patterns which makes him feel 'he has lost control'. The solution is to get rid of the 'pain in the ass' code or thinking.

I know it seems too simplistic. Why would the doctors not recommend this? The answer is because they do not understand the simplicity. And secondly, they cannot get rid of the code for you—you have to do it for yourself. Which leads to the question **HOW**? And that question, my dear Alita, I will not answer for you—you will have to discover the answer for yourself!"

"Tell me more about the boomerang effect," Alita continued because she instinctually understood part of her quest lay in understanding Sam's description of this metaphor.

Sam smiled, "If you go to an event and everything goes wrong, but you relax and enjoy it, this is totally different than if you get angry. This is one level of the boomerang effect. When I was on the mountain with 'One Who Knows', I visually saw the boomerang effect—each and every thought *flew out* immediately and continuously from inside my being, and instantly rebounded or *flew back* directly into my spiritual essence. I imagine, Eastern mystics would describe this as an aspect of 'Karma' (cause and effect), except I would call it 'immediate karma'. I saw something like this—take a rubber band and stretch it with your thumb and let it go. The rebound effect demonstrates why humans are resilient in the present moment, even when the most difficult of situations are experienced, but please don't ask me to explain any further what I saw, because the experience was a fleeting and dramatic split second."

"Sam, how do you see help being provided for my People?"

"Alita, it is actually quite simple! There must be a different answer than in the past—today (because it is not exclusively a Native world), it has to include the healing power of the Great Spirit + the spiritual guidance to present-day mental and psychological pressures, or what some call, the workings of the little mind.

For instance, you have deep respect for the mystical energy of the Spirit inside the Sweat Lodge—and this is very wise of you—and you are equally aware of the sacred healing powers that exist within every human being. However, you still need to learn more on how to introduce others to their true Self once they walk out of the Sweat Lodge door and re-enter their illusionary life of stress and low moods. Once you truly have *seen* the connection between the spiritual and psychological worlds, your heightened state of consciousness automatically will provide guidance to your People."

"That makes sense," Alita commented. She gave a loving touch on Sam's hand and decided to get some sleep.

Finally after an exhausting five-hour flight they arrived in Puerto Vallerta airport. Clearing customs was relatively easy; then they walked with their luggage past many Mexicans salesmen trying to sell timeshares to the tourists coming off the planes. These smiling salesmen even suggested they were the bus rides to the hotel of the tourist, but of course, they were not.

The air conditioned Greyhound tour bus was sitting just outside of the doors of the airport, waiting to take the busload of

Canadians to the resort of Decameron los Cocos. The temperature was about 27°C and felt amazing to both of them. As it turned out, their whole time in Mexico was just about right with perfectly sunny days and a heat which was hot but not oppressive. This is typical of Mexico in late April.

While they were waiting for the bus to leave, Sam gave her a printout of a past tourist comment on their resort. It said, "For one who wishes to experience the close proximity of Mexicans, this is for you! The multitude of families native to the country, which share your space will uplift you! Great to hear the language spoken, to observe how the Mexicans play with their children. The staff at the Los Cocos…unbeatable! The accommodation was great, food was good and we got to see the real Mexico. Actually the town that Los Cocos is located in, Rincon de Guayabitos was bigger then we thought, pleasant surprise. There were lots of restaurants, shops and plenty to do. Went to the next town, La Panetta on Thursday, their market day, and had a blast. The rooster has to go, he crows any time he wants, especially in the early morning."

Alita giggled and said to Sam, "Sounds like fun, but look out for that rooster!"

The one and a half hour ride was uneventful, especially as Alita and Sam were tired. They noticed for the first half-hour or so, there was the usual hustle and bustle related to the faster pace of the successful tourist town of Puerto Vallerta. They also noticed the squalor and dilapidated housing and stores. However, as the ride continued, they saw dry vegetation requiring water intermittent with construction messes and whatever. As they got closer to their destination, the vegetation grew more intense with trees and open spaces. It was definitely a quieter and more serene atmosphere than Puerto Vallerta. Alita and Sam smiled to each other and instinctively relaxed.

Finally, the bus pulled off the highway down a road leading to the town and the bay of Rincon de Guayabitos. After one major turn they had arrived at their hotel. It looked more impressive than they expected and were greeted by the smiling concierge. Their luggage was unloaded with Sam giving one of the men a $1 tip. Initially, the resort turned out to be a bit confusing as it was not one hotel but five buildings located in close proximity to each other, but not necessarily right next to each other. Los Cocos One, Two, Three, Four and Five were the building names, with three restaurants and various activities and services located in each of the five buildings.

They waited at the reception for the initial confusion of tourist registration to subside and eventually their number was called. They were quickly given a key and a plastic band strapped to their wrist, which identified them as an 'all inclusive guest'. Sam said "Buenos amigo" and smiles were exchanged. They had been assigned number 4314 in Los Cocos 4; their bags would be brought to their room a bit later. They casually walked out of the dreamy entrance, and saw one of the four swimming pools of the resort, along with colorful flowers and trees with steps leading up to the top floor where their room was situated. The booking agent had told them they would have a tiny room and while they had requested a view, because of the low cost of their vacation package, they had been told not to expect that.

On the fourth floor, they stopped at their door and looked directly behind them, which was open to a surrealistic backdrop of a huge forest area with a majestic giant Catholic Cross residing over the scenic view at the very top of the treed and shrubbed hill. It was a serene and religious moment. Then, they twisted around, turned the key to their room and opened the door. To their surprise, it was the largest room anyone could imagine. Alita quickly ran in and shut off the air conditioning, as it was blaring with a huge noise and blasting cold air. The room was immense. There were two double beds, which they pushed together. It was a Mexican design with its pink and green colors, cement pillars and a ceiling that looked like a roof. The view was spectacular, although not as impressive as the one Alita had experienced in Cancun.

They looked at each other and said, "Not too shabby," and laughed. Later, they noticed the resort was indeed Mexican in flavor with at least 70% of the residents being Mexican families with their kids.

Sam slept in one bed, Alita in the other resting for a half-hour before dinner. Then they walked slowly hand in hand to Cocos 5 where their dinner reservation had been made at one of the two restaurants on the beach. They met a married couple; the man was from Alberta, Canada and the wife from Cuba. They proved to be excellent company. He was a devout hater of Fidel Castro, while the wife patiently sat disapproving of his exaggerations and narrow-minded conclusions about Cuba. She had a fire in her eye that Alita could not help but admire. She loved living in Alberta with her husband, but Alita couldn't help noticing she passionately loved her homeland as well. The buffet was surprisingly scrumptious with a huge variety of breads, salads, main courses and deserts, and of course all the free alcoholic and non-alcoholic drinks they could want. Sam ordered a dark Mexican beer with his meal while Alita had some Kahlua with her coffee after the meal. While they continued to have the occasional alcoholic drink at dinner time, their limited alcohol consumption proved to be a rarity in this resort for they ended up drinking mostly pineapple juice during the day while the other Mexican and Canadian tourists were devouring large amounts of alcohol to their hearts content. The beach setting was lovely. They had begun their travels in style.

Chapter 27
The Sundance Ceremony

The next day, after a delicious breakfast highlighted by the world's best coffee and omelets freshly prepared and cooked by a smiling Mexican lady chef, Alita and Sam walked down to their hotel's beach. It was full of activity by the employees and guests of the hotel, and included lawn chairs to sit on, water activities, and a picturesque scene of boats overlooking the calm Mexican waters. Vendors with umbrellas, hats, food snacks, candy, jewellery and a host of other treats were walking by with their push carts or hand held items. Behind them was a hotel cantina, which served free alcoholic or non-alcoholic drinks, and Mexican or American snacks. During the hottest part of the afternoon, Sam and Alita happily gobbled three gratuitous delicious ice cream cones of various flavors and toppings, which were prepared and served from a large cart by several young hotel staff members.

While relaxing in the midday sun, Alita mentioned she had been privileged to assist a dancer in a Sundance ceremony in the interior of British Columbia, a week prior to meeting Sam. She revealed how powerful her experience had been, and with Sam's encouragement and questions, she continued her story.

"Sam, as it was my first Sundance and a dream of mine to go, I walked into this sacred ceremony with a pleased heart. The drive up to Merritt, BC took about four to five hours, and I arrived to an idyllic setting of an isolated small valley nestled between rolling desert hills on the left and thick green trees on the right side, with a small creek running through the valley to wash off the dust and heat of the day. There were about 400 Natives camping with tents, trailers, trucks and cars. This setting provided us with all the peace and privacy any Sundance could wish or hope for. The weather was hot during the day and cold at night. Naturally, a kitchen was set up to feed all the People.

I was made welcome by numerous Sundancers and camped with the People from Vancouver. I was introduced to the British Columbia Chief and various others including a remarkable 12 year old boy who I learned was Chief of the younger ones and destined to be Chief of the Sundance when he was older. He greatly impressed me with his confidence and majestic air.

Sam, let me express a few memorable moments before I describe a bit of the Sundance ceremony.

First of all, there were five Sundance Chiefs from different areas, lead by the wisest, the Chief from Minnesota. Normally the different Chiefs have difficulty in agreeing with each other, but at this ceremonial gathering they were in accord and this union brought great peace and harmony in the gathering.

Then, there was another historical moment, when a dancer of two spirits (gay) was honored with a special ceremony. After the one hour ceremony ended, he was welcome on either side of the lodge or arbor, as one side had only men and the other side women. Since he had not previously been allowed to dance at other Sundance's, I took this as a historical breakthrough. One of the wise men talked to the group of dancers and helpers inside the arbor and said, 'We call him a man of two spirits, but it is my understanding on talking with the Chiefs of the Sundance that there is only one spirit. We are all born with one spirit and then we display it in the manner we choose'.

To me, Sam, this was very wise and is my understanding as well."

Sam nodded in agreement with Alita on this point.

Alita continued, "At the Sundance, a non-native Royal Canadian Mounted Policeman (RCMP) was invited to attend the ceremony in full uniform. He was honored to be there, and told me how pleased it made him feel, because, not so many years ago, the Sundance was banned in Canada. In his talk, the Minnesota Chief mentioned how happy they were to have this officer at the ceremony, as it was a necessary healing event for the People to forgive the RCMP. Many years ago the Stoney Mountain Penitentiary in Manitoba was built to exclusively hold Sundance participants, and it is ironic that to this day about 80% of its inmates is Native.

Another impressive aspect of the gathering was the strength of character and astuteness of the People. Many were professors at universities, movie directors, psychologists, teachers and lawyers. To their credit, they still carry their traditions with them while entering the white man's world of money and success. Their self-esteem and personal understanding of life is wise and powerful, and proves to me Natives can be successful and spiritual at the same time. In fact, it is a model and a requirement for success, in my mind, for Natives.

I met a psychologist whom I talked to intensely for two hours, and we are going to get together when I return to Vancouver. He liked how simply I explained the workings of the Mind."

Sam suddenly became animated, passionately urging Alita to maintain contact with this psychologist. "Great possibilities can arise when working with the wiser practitioners of the helping professions."

Alita nodded and continued her storytelling about the Sundance. "The ceremonies were gripping, and I have come to believe they are either the most powerful, or close to the most powerful, of all sacred ceremonies for our People. Basically, a huge arbor or lodge is built of tree branches whereby the dancers are hidden in a corridor of branches around the huge arbor. In the center of the lodge is a magnificent sacred tree driven into the ground; the helpers stand around this while facing an open sky. A big drum and four (4) drummers are situated on the Northern side where the Minnesota Chief also drums and/or guides the talks and ceremonies. Then the hanging, dragging and piercing takes place."

Sam had never attended a Sundance, so Alita talked about the three different ceremonies and her experiences with these. "The hangings are when the men are pierced in the shoulders or breasts and hung on the sacred tree. At first, I found it nauseating and had trouble with this in my mind, but after a while I relaxed and experienced the power of the Moment—the giving by the Dancer of his flesh to the Great Spirit as (s)he experienced an altered and majestic state of consciousness. One Sundancer described it to me as seeing the energy flow from the Great Sacred Tree through the ropes into the dancer and at other times flow back through the tree and explode out at the top. When one sees or feels this energy, the ceremony ceases to be barbaric. It becomes serene and sacred. During a pause in the ceremonies, I squeezed my arms around the Tree, and felt its immense power.

Later, I talked to a young 19 year old who had pierced for the first time. After his skin is pierced around his shoulders, the dancer drags his feet backwards pulling as hard as possible on the rope, which is attached to the Tree and this piercing. The dancer actually leans backward and sometimes the piercings pulls out of the skin. Sage acts as a healing agent as it is put on the pulled skin, immediately after the Sundancer's ceremony. I asked him what his experience had been like, and he answered, 'Unexplainable', as he indicated the heavenly state he experienced. I mentioned to him that anything worthwhile in life is unexplainable and we nodded in agreement to each other.

Later, I walked around the outside of the arbor as my friend dragged four buffalo skulls with a rope pierced to his back. I could hear the buffalo herd running with him, especially as he dragged past the drummers who were beating feverishly inside the arbor.

Later, the wife of the Minnesota Chief explained to the women that it is important to support your man, but never forget 'Who you are as a Woman. In fact, as long as you know who you are, you will never have to suffer abuse or other travesties from your man'. I could not help but be impressed by the Power the Chief's wife exuded to the 24 Woman Dancers who would pierce later in the ceremony. Her message was very powerful, because as you know Sam, there is a lot of abuse by men, to their women in the Native world.

There were many other powerful healing experiences I experienced at the Sundance, but I think that will do for now," said Alita as she kissed Sam fully on the mouth and let him know how pleased she was to be with him on this exotic holiday. Another scrumptious dinner awaited!

Chapter 28
The Nagual

After two days, Sam developed a bit of a stomach problem, for he liked to try all of the free food, some of which was interesting looking, but spiced and cooked to Mexican tastes.

There were palm trees as he looked out the sliding door. It was tranquil with the noise of early morning birds chirping and cars passing by far below. He experienced a tired relaxation, a slight headache, a fever and a touch of dysentery running through his body

Alita lovingly gave him an Imodium pill, and after sleeping for several hours, he awoke feeling energized. He mentioned to Alita he was going for a walk on the beach to clear his head and he would see her a bit later. She smiled and nodded.

At the beach, he sleepily glanced around and saw an intriguing looking older Mexican sitting on a chair, wearing the oldest and most worn out looking cowboy hat Sam had ever seen. Sam slowly walked over and introduced himself.

The smiling Mexican said in surprisingly good English, "Hi, I am Miguel León. I live by myself in the outskirts of the Huichol Community of Nayarit about two hours from here. I would guess there are approximately 8,000 Huichol scattered throughout the Sierra Madre mountains; they are a peaceful people, they have no known history of war," and thus began a relationship which was to change the destiny of Alita and Sam's holiday.

Later, Sam returned to the room and casually mentioned to Alita, "I have just met a Toltec shaman."

Alita looked up with surprise and asked, "What did he say?"

"He gave me a bit of a history lesson at first. The Toltecs were a Pre-Columbian Native American people who dominated much of central Mexico between the 10th and 12th century AD: their leaders were thought of as being alongside deities. Many future rulers of other cultures, including Mayan leaders and Aztec emperors, claimed to be descended from the Toltecs. These cultures often revered them and copied their legends, art, buildings and religion

However, unlike the Toltecs, who are known as women and men of knowledge, the Aztecs and the Mayans abused their power, not understanding the records of the Toltec teachings found at the pyramids. The Toltecs taught of the *giving of the open heart* to the Sun. This spiritual tradition concerned the development of what is called a 'divinized heart' within a human being whereas the Aztecs took that to mean performing human sacrifice because they believed the ritual of giving a human life would be the most valuable and highest form of appeasing the Sky Gods, thus avoiding famines and other disasters.

Many have spoken of the Toltec as a nation or a race, but in fact, the Toltec were scientists and artists who formed a society to explore and conserve the spiritual knowledge and practices of the ancient ones. It may seem peculiar that they combined the secular with the sacred, but the Toltec considered science and spirit to be one and the same since all energy, whether material or ethereal, was derived from the One source and influenced by the same universal laws.

The history of the Toltec culture at Teotihuacan (in the first half of the 1st millennium CE, the largest city in the pre-Columbian Americas; it may have had more than 100,000 inhabitants placing it among the largest cities of the world in this period, and is famous for its pyramid structures) is shrouded in mystery. It is speculated that around the year 500 AD the Toltec Naguals had learned how to transmute, to go through the Black Feathered Sun to the place of creation."

Alita mentioned she had heard of this phrase and said to Sam, "The Black Feathered Sun is a Plains Indian symbol with stylized feathers pointing both inwards and outwards; inward towards the center and outward to the circumference. It combines the symbols of the sun and the eagle and depicts the universe; the center; solar power; radiation of power; and majesty."

"Interesting, this connection is," said Sam in his Star Wars Yoda voice.

"Then Miguel León looked into my eyes and stated that he is a Nagual, a teacher of Toltec wisdom." He smiled as he could see how fascinated I was with his talk.

"My teachings will fascinate any man, such as you, who is searching for a stronger understanding of Truth," added Miguel León.

Sam continued to paraphrase the Nagual, "The ancient Toltec knew that our perception of reality was just a point of view. We can all dream a new dream and live a life of freedom. To say it plainly, nagual is not the powerful guru or shaman, but is half of the reality in which we live and half of our own nature."

Does that make sense Alita?"

"Yes, it is how I see the Oneness—the power of All integrated with our own Personal Power. In many ways, I see the Holy Spirit or the Holy Ghost of Christianity exactly like this."

Sam then continued telling his story about Miguel León. "Toltec knowledge arises from the same essential unity of truth as all the sacred esoteric traditions around the world. While it is not a religion, it does honor all the spiritual masters who have taught on the earth. It does embrace spirit, and would most accurately be described as a way of life and the ready accessibility of *happiness and love.*

Alita interrupted and said, "He sounds a lot like Carlos Castaneda, a writer who fascinated the hippies of the 70's with his experiences with hallucegenic drugs and encounters with two enlightened sorcerers, Don Juan and Don Genero. Carlos also used the word 'nagual' in describing the world of spirit. Perhaps his experiences had a Toltec influence?"

Sam replied, "I do not know but I am not interested in Carlos Castaneda at this moment. I always trust my intuition regarding people, and this is telling me I want to spend more time with this insightful Nagual."

Alita asked, "How do you see Miguel León in comparison to the man you call 'One Who Knows'?"

Sam replied, "It is an irrelevant comparison. At this present moment, Miguel León is in my reality and I know I am enjoying the exploration into his world and how he describes 'The World of Spirit'. He has much to teach me, just like you, Alita, have much to teach me about my heart. Alita blushed slightly; then she could not help but smile, a big radiant smile that almost matched the sunset and gave Sam a warm glow.

Sam continued talking about the Nagual. "Miguel León then began some personal teachings and left the history lesson behind. He suggested all human thoughts from the mind are lies. Lies such as 'I'm not perfect', 'I lack self-esteem or confidence in myself' or 'Why don't other people see life as I see it' create a story which we use to justify our point of view and often our pitiful existence. We are continually fooling ourselves by repeating our or other human's lies to ourselves, and worse yet, we pretend they are true. The more we believe these lies, the more our life becomes like a dream or what the Toltec call *dreaming*. You and I would call these lies by the psychological term—ego.

Now, when we, as the dreamer, see we are living as a liar, then we experience there are two worlds; the *first* world in which we lie and justify our lies to ourselves versus the *second* world of spirit where silence and the stillness is a reality. Then we can be free because we know what we are, or what kind of freedom we are looking for. The world Toltec means 'artist of the spirit' and as such, we can dream without limitation or ego restriction. After all, Miguel León emphasized, just as 'One Who Knows' did, *'It's a World of Thought.'*

"Alita," he suggested, "We can transform the dream of our life by changing our agreements and beliefs of our world. The goal of the Toltec is to reclaim our divinity and become one with God. Of course, you and I have a multifaceted fascination with this theme.

Alita, I know this is sudden but I must go now and spend some time with Miguel León. I know you are disappointed, but this is something I must do. I will return in a few days."

He said this as he hugged and gave her a caring and loving look. "I will return on Wednesday and we will go the Beach club together."

She nodded; he opened the door and left.

Alita was hurt and wondered if Sam really cared for her. He was always leaving her alone and she wondered about their relationship? Her mind continued to chirp with these doubts.

Then she smiled, and remembered a line from a Leonard Cohen song, "There ain't no cure for love," she laughed and said to herself, "I am a big girl and I am on holiday here in exotic Mexico. I cannot change Sam and I want to enjoy my holiday. Besides Sam is not Chaim, he lives in a secure mind and I believe I can trust him." She relaxed, laughed again and decided to go downstairs for a coffee.

Chapter 29
Alita's Time Alone

Very early next morning she awoke and looked out the window. For the first time, it was overcast, but the setting was still picturesque as it was at rest before the noisy and hectic activity of the awakened Mexican day.

As she looked out from the fourth floor balcony, the sprawling mountains in the far background lacing the huge bay greeted her, accompanied by the immense gray waterspan and majestic palm trees. To the far left, at the top of a hill overlooking the bay like a lord, sat an opulent and expensive restaurant. Its colors reminded Alita of a construction site. Below to the left, was the figure eight pool with a cute purple bridge in its middle. Four birds flew directly in front of her view with twenty or thirty others farther back. The Tijeretas (pronounced scissors) were white chested with a wide wing span and fairly sharp beaks with fan like tails. Alita loved their free flowing movements.

The resort with its five buildings had colors of pastel purple, deep red, pale pink, and shades of green and white. In front of her panoramic view was an apartment roof with clothes being hung out to dry. Beside this was a half completed apartment looking dismantled or bombed. Beside this was an older dumpy building called Los Palmos Bungalows with a store at street level playing Mexican music all day long and blankets sticking out of the top window. In Alita's courtyard, beautiful palm trees, red flowers and scrubs silhouetted the property. A happy black bird sat on a tree. The Spanish tile roof of the building below the balcony was splattered with loose and broken tile where some repairs had probably been undertaken. The resort's roof was a bit of a mess, even though the resort was immaculately clean in every other respect.

This was Mexico, a paradox of contrasts—exotically beautiful, but a bit tough to take sometimes. The people were poor but happy and did they ever like to drink alcohol. The workers at the resort earn, approximately, $98 plus tips in two weeks working twelve hour shifts. They often lived in homes without doors and windows. Many Mexican fathers walked around with their huge family units lovingly carrying their youngest children. These family feelings were similar to those in her People.

Breakfast would begin soon and Alita began to wonder if Sam and she would ever get closer—she felt they were so far apart, but he seemed to prefer it this way.

One half hour later, the sun broke through, the nonstop music began from across the street, the boats in the harbor woke up, the big yellow party boat in the bay got ready for the Mexican crowd and the grayness dissolved into blue sky and ocean.

Alita looked down from the four-story balcony and saw the daily Mexican workers below, talking and going about their jobs. The street became busy with cars and locals. Occasional speakers in cars loudly announced something in Mexican, trying to incite some interest about something wonderful for the locals to spend their hard earned money on. In the neighboring town of La Panetta, it was the same. When she biked along their stoned roads, Alita saw a truck pulling a cage of four of the most sleepy and worn out lions she had ever seen going through the town advertising and yelling on loud speakers about the local circus in town.

Later, Alita wanted to get some quiet away from the constant noise and music of her complex, so she decided to walk down the beach to what looked like a secluded end of the bay. As she walked into the soothing water up to her ankles, the buildings on her left became more worn down. She passed old restaurants and drinking holes with a different style of music and atmosphere from her classier resort. Nearer to the end of the land, there were two or three beautiful homes overlooking the bay. On the secluded beach, a few Mexican families were eating and enjoying the relative tranquility. The music from her abode could be heard, but it was muted and softer. Then she walked to the edge of the landscape wanting to see the many palm trees and rocks. As she looked up, she realized the palm trees surprisingly hid a militia camp. This obviously was hidden for a reason; probably as a protection against the shenanigans of the Mexicans, especially when they were under the influence of alcohol. Previously, a Canadian gal had casually mentioned that when she went to a local disco, she saw 10-year-old Mexican boys looking for girls and drinking like fish. However, Alita's assumption proved incorrect. The hidden militia camp primarily served as a deterrent against drugs and the many banditos of Mexico.

Later, Alita had a lovely dinner with a rich retired Albertan who told her the owners of the resort were Columbian. He imagined it was because the militia was keeping on top of everything that this resort was so successful. At the same time, both he and Alita could not deny their appreciation of the beauty of the Mexican people. Alita noted they seemed to explode with pleasure at the slightest sign. For instance, when she joined in dancing with a handsome Mexican staff member of the hotel, an older Mexican man exploded with excited Ai ja ja's and glitter in his eyes.

"What was it in the Indian People that needed so much regulation and why did they self-destruct so easily?" She would have to ask Sam.

Her mind drifted back to being on the beach and she now could see a truck and many militia personnel. One imposing and tough looking militia hombre with a huge rifle draped over his shoulder definitely started to eye her and slowly walked down the embankment in her general direction, creeping forward constantly and ever so slowly. An uncomfortable feeling guided Alita to pick up her few things and slowly but surely walk back in the general direction of the resort. What a strange feeling! The militia obviously did not want tourists spying on them.

The Mexicans seemed to have many rules and she noticed they often distrusted another's words. For example, if she had to bring a boogie board back at a certain time they always emphasized to her that she must obey the rules. However, these were minor inconveniences and Alita grew to love her time alone in the sun and enjoyed the interesting and varied daily evening entertainment at the resort.

Besides she was looking forward to hearing about Sam's adventures and spending tomorrow with him at the Beach Club.

Chapter 30
The Beach Club

At around 9:30 in the morning Sam appeared at the door of their suite with a sheepish smile on his face and said, "A perfect day for the Beach Club". They hugged and felt the warmth and intimacy between each other, then walked down the stairs together to the front entrance where the bus would be taking them, ten other Canadians and one Mexican family to the Beach Club. Both of them were in a tranquil mood, and made a silent pact to enjoy their time together, rather than discuss his past adventures.

The ride was about twenty-five minutes down the same road they had come from Puerto Vallerta, but this time the bus turned into a small village where there were no hotels. The bus drove past a church stopping right at the sand of the beach, and when they got off the bus; their eyes were greeted with a spectacular beach, which reminded Alita of the beaches in Hawaii. The beach was miles and miles of sand with huge crushing waves flowing onto the shore, the turquoise blue ocean swept out forever. There were a few people sitting sporadically along the miles of beach.

The beach club turned out to be a designated area on the beach with many comfortable lawn chairs covered by thatched straw roofs to protect one from the rays of the sun. Additionally, there was one larger thatched roof area where lunch was being prepared and would be eaten. Beside this was a small area where the 'king of the alcoholic cocktail makers' resided with his bottles of delicious and powerful concoctions; all the tourists eagerly ordered their favorite alcoholic drinks. Sam and Alita smiled as they followed the initial crowd and ordered their delicious iced pineapple juices, and once again, they were the only ones drinking non-alcoholic drinks.

At noon, lunch was served, with tasty Mexican delights such as salsa, salads, chicken in a sauce plus hamburger and chips for the North American palate. Two older caballeros with a guitar and fiddle came up to the tourists asking if they would like a song for a few pesos. The Mexican family pulled out some loose change and the music began. Before a few seconds passed, the Mexican Dad was up dancing with the musicians. Before Alita could blink, Sam was clapping to the music. The Mexican Dad started to sing and encouraged by his wife and two teenage sons, Sam rose and laughingly danced in tune with the Mexicans. All were lifted by the feelings and Alita could see Sam wasn't doing it consciously or with effort, he was doing it because this was 'who he is'.

After lunch, Sam and Alita went for a long walk along the beach. It was one of their favorite moments, both of them valuing the peaceful walk in an idyllic setting. Their time together was gentle, soothing and romantic.

Walking on the beach, Sam looked into the ocean and yelled, "I am a human being, you are the Universe" and the Power poured into his soul.

On returning to their beach spot, Sam and Alita looked out into the ocean and saw one macho male Canadian who obviously loved the raw physical nature of the ocean; they joined him in boogie boarding on the perfect waves. Each wave was different in strength and height, and when well chosen, the ride into the beach was 'awesome'. Alita swore, as Sam caught a wave, she could see him laughing like a little kid, enjoying the moment in totality and surrendering to the beauty and power of the thunderous waves of the ocean. She did likewise.

Then, after boogie boarding for half an hour, Sam sat on his boogie board on the beach as huge waves poured onto the sand. From time to time the waves swamped the sitting Sam, who laughed and laughed from the experience.

Alita went for another pineapple juice and talked to the Mexican bartender about whose cocktail making abilities all the tourists were raving about. She mentioned that Canadians and Mexicans have one quality in common, and the Mexican bartender eagerly looked up with wonder.

She said, "They have great fighting spirit." The Mexican people are known as great boxers, and she had no doubt they were warriors who would fight to the bitter end. She mentioned she had seen a boxing match between Marquez and Pacquio, and they fought right to the end, even though Marquez was knocked down.

"Yah," they both agreed, "two great warriors fighting for *pride*"—a pride she had seen many times in her own people.

Later, around three o'clock the bus driver arrived on the beach and announced he would be taking everyone back in fifteen minutes; the bus was parked in the lane of the first street. Of course, he would have to have a few drinks before driving back to the hotel and he eagerly attacked these. Sam and Alita remembered seeing a church near to where the bus was parked. They picked up their belongings and walked over to the petite place of worship.

It was made of stucco, decorated like a Moorish temple with a round roof protruding across the higher section and a cross on top of this. Inside, it felt like a Catholic Church. The sitting area for the masses consisted of several plain benches, but the front, where all would face, was impressive—just as Alita had seen in other Mexican churches. In this case, there was a lion, the Virgin Mary and, of course, Christ on the cross, all tastefully and religiously carved overlooking the pulpit where the Sunday sermon would be delivered.

They smiled at each other with appreciation, and casually walked back to the bus where they were driven back to their hotel. Sam expressed his regret and 'sorryness' to Alita for not spending the last night with her, as he had promised to return to Miguel León for the evening, but would be coming back tomorrow morning for their last breakfast before catching the airplane back to Vancouver.

As Alita walked back to her hotel room, alone once again, she looked up to the mighty Catholic cross overlooking the resort. She had heard it was 265 steps to the top and she had promised herself she would take this mighty hike before her trip was over, as several other guests had mentioned the view was breathtaking. However, at this moment, she did not feel like the climb and looked up at the power of the Cross. She prayed with all her sorrow and despair, asking God to help her, because "She knew she could not make things happen. Why is life 'muy loco?'" She would wait for a sign to help her in understanding what would happen between Sam and her. Peace walked into her soul, as she felt her faith join with God's abundance and love.

Chapter 31
The Final Morning

The next morning Alita was up early. She was sitting in the stoned floor area beside the restaurant, drinking the delicious Mexican coffee; green tables on the veranda overlooking grass and palm trees, and the early morning birds crisply singing their songs of delight of being alive. A quiet mist permeated the complex. As it was early morning, the servers and preparers of food were happily chirping among themselves, pleasantly busy getting the tables ready for 7:00 a.m., while cheerfully and enjoyably talking among themselves. They worked long hours for low pay, but recognized this resort was a pleasant place to work.

Coconuts from the palm trees hung full of liquid clear syrup, which the locals drank, drilling a clean hole through the coconut's tough outer shell to access its refreshing liquid. The tree above the veranda held about 40 coconuts. The locals would cut down other coconuts for local consumption and/or sell them on the street or the beaches.

Sam arrived for breakfast.

They hugged and lightly kissed. Alita asked about Miguel León.

Sam began, "He talked about many aspects of life being spiritual. One topic I personally liked was if we see a tree, we just don't just see the tree. We qualify, describe, or have an opinion about the tree. Maybe, we like the tree or we don't like the tree. It turns out our opinion about the tree is a story of our own creation. So, as many wise men have said, once we analyze and judge what we perceive, it is no longer real; it is an illusion. This is what the Toltec call 'dreaming'. The Toltec believe humans are living in a dream and the mind dreams when the brain is both asleep and awake.

I especially enjoyed his metaphor that we humans are almost always wearing a mask. When I asked what he meant, he said, 'Sometimes, when you go to work, even though you are tired and discouraged, you are smiling. You only pretend to be happy. This smile is a mask. Remove the mask and see 'Who you are', and this will set you free.

I definitely have become more relaxed about all of life by hanging out with Miguel León. It is amazing that many people believe stress is caused by something *'outside of their own thinking'*. While I understood this before, I have become more fully aware that all aspects of stress are a man-made thinking phenomenon; yet only a small percentage of humanity understands this.

If we *slow our thinking down*, we walk towards the Silence we all yearn for, towards a stress-less reality and a world of happiness and contentment. I have come to realize 'One Who Knows' was guiding me 'home' &/or to my Spiritual Identity. By entering this world of Inner Silence or Universal Consciousness, all personal problems miraculously disappear."

Then Sam changed topics and said, "When you return to Vancouver, I will introduce you to 'One Who Knows' and maybe he can complete your training and understanding on how to help all your uncles and aunties. Miguel León told me, 'You, Alita, have what you need right now'. Go home and experience this. I must stay. It is my destiny to learn from Miguel León for a while."

"I am sure we will meet again and when I return to Canada, I will look forward to the continuation of our relationship."

Alita looked at him, and said, "Do we have a relationship?"

Sam affectionately said, "Yes, I love you!"...

"But you must return to Canada. See you in a couple of weeks or so. If we are lucky, we can share a pipe ceremony with Johnny at that time." As Sam smiled tenderly, he rose from the table.

Alita responded, "Muy bien."

Chapter 32
The Wolf Revisited

The wolf is the teacher and nurturer. Their spirit represents the lessons to be learned from thoughtful contemplation of the world and the experiences that life brings. They signify willingness both to lead the way and to be led. The wolf is a symbol of great strength.

In Chapter 15, the child asked the Cherokee Elder, *"Which wolf will win?"* and he answered, *"The one you feed."*

And Now the child asked the Cherokee Elder, *"How do you feed the wolf?"*

And he answered, *"With our thought(s)."*

Then after a time of silence, the child tugged at the pant leg of the Elder and asked another question, *"Grandfather, which wolf, the white one or the black one is stronger?"*

The Grandfather stated, *"Inside you is the strongest wolf in the world, open your heart to this fact, and you will experience the combined power of both wolves. Creator gave you the power of connection to the* **wolf within**. *This connection is your ultimate destiny as a warrior, a healer and a human being."*

"Grandfather, what is my destiny?" And Grandfather stated, *"Whatever you choose."*

Alita concluded by saying, *"READERS, stop complaining about your destiny—if you do not like it, forgive yourself and allow change to occur. Begin to live a life full of contentment and happiness, it will guide you home. That, my friends, is a money-back guarantee because it is indeed your destiny."*

Mark Twain said,
"My life has been very difficult. Fortunately most of it isn't true."

Chapter 33

The Prophecy of the Wolf Vision

Alita's pipe had been idle for many months. Lately, the pipe had been calling to her, so one Saturday morning; she untied the sacred bundle, which contained her sacred pipe, the stem and bowl wrapped separately in red spirit cloth.

She laid her small brown suede Mexican blanket on the floor. It was designed with a slanted square signifying the four directions of Native spirituality, a leather flower nestled in each of the four corners. She placed upon the blanket, a fish made out of deer antler given to her by a wise Native healer; a woolen black spider from the maker of the pipe; a little carved boat made by one of her clients in a remote reservation; sacred herbs from California for the smoke; all together with the joined pipe. She loved the pipe ceremony with all her sentimental pieces on the blanket.

To those sacred items already on the blanket, she added some sage she had collected from Lillooet for 'smudging', a smudge bowl of abalone given to her by a Blackfoot pipe carrier and an embroidered eagle feather given by the pipe carver himself.

Native Elders had taught her that before a person can be healed, or to heal another, one must be cleansed of any bad feelings, negative thoughts, bad spirits or negative energy. They must be cleansed physically, mentally and spiritually. This helps the healing to come through in a clear way, without being distorted or sidetracked by 'negative 'stuff' in either the healer or the client. The Elders said all ceremonies, tribal or private, must be entered into with a good heart so they can pray, sing, and walk in a sacred manner, and be helped by the spirits to enter the sacred realm.

Native people throughout the world use herbs to accomplish this. The common ceremony of 'smudging' is to burn certain herbs, then to take the smoke in one's hands and finally rub or brush it over the body and/or ceremonial objects.

In preparation, Alita lit the sage in the bowl and watched the smoke curl and wind its way leisurely to the ceiling. Then with the eagle feather, she drew the smoke to her and brushed it over her body and all the objects on the blanket, including the joined pipe, while she prayed.

She then began the pipe ceremony as she had learned it, praying to the Four Directions, Father Sky, Mother Earth and Creator. After a half-hour prayer, she began to smoke the pipe. As she finished, the Medicine Wolf song came into her mind. Once again her spirit helper—The Wolf—appeared before her eyes. This time its demeanor had softened. Its look expressed friendliness and sageness. In fact, Alita felt the Wolf looked regal, like she imagined the Three Wise men might look as they followed the sacred star towards Bethlehem. The Wolf once again entered her being and she felt its physical and spiritual strength integrate deep within her soul. All at once, a Vision of the Wolf reappeared and began speaking:

"And so it is

The 'One Who Knows' will teach you about the sacred workings of the Spirit world; and this knowledge will alleviate all the suffering of your Aunties and Uncles. In fact, the three Principles of the Spirit world have the unlimited potential to totally alleviate all the suffering of mankind; that is every known mental illness, every psychological problem that exists in the world today, and all alcohol and drug addictions. When the doctoring fields recognize this, it will help heal millions of people and change psychology forever. Then, the Native healers and psychologists will tap into the true world of Spirit and Mind.

"But, what are the three Spiritual Principles?" thought Alita.

The Spiritwolf answered, "'The One Who Knows' has the answer to your question.

I say to you, The Native world was always instinctual and spiritual. However, our Native People gradually became lost when they lost their self-esteem and pride in themselves, and because they suffered the ill effects of an idle mind. Their mental problems are exactly the same as the Non-Native world; just the appearance of the problems is different.

Now is the time for you, Alita, to venture forth in the world and help in whatever small way you are capable. There will be many wiser teachers guiding the world in this direction, but with your help, they will be stronger. Also, many Native People will only listen to you. It is the magic of wisdom, for spiritual knowledge heals those who listen.

Of what you take, you must share. Share and complete the circle. Your heart will be blessed beyond words.

The Spiritwolf ended by saying, "All my relatives, it is indeed so!"

The Wolf then disappeared leaving Alita alone and smiling. She now had a potential 'Gift to Mankind'.

She knew the prophecy of the Wolf was another mystical gift and her journey had just begun.

She thought of Sam!!

The End

Bibliography

1, 2 From Sydney Banks and his books Missing Link, Enlightened Gardener Revisited, + Second Chance + In Quest of the Pearl

4 From Wikipedia, the free encyclopedia

5 Mana from http"Mana"from http://hawaiianlanguage.com/ mana.html. Supernatural or divine power, miraculous power. Mana is divinely-given power and authority. All of life possesses mana to some degree.

6 "Sephirot"from Wikipedia, the free encyclopedia Sephirot or "enumerations," in the Kabbalah of Judaism, are the ten attributes that God (who is referred to as Aur Ain Soph, "Limitless Light, Light Without End") created through which he can manifest not only the physical but the metaphysical universe.

The first three attributes are:
Keter is the Great Nothingness, and this quality of Nothingness is the closest that we human beings can come to a true understanding of the divine—or "God is all, all is God"

Chochmah is Divine Thought or the flash of inspiration—when an insight is experienced from the unknown.
Binah is the third sephiroth of the Kabbalistic Tree of Life. It is intuition and enlightenment of consciousness

7 From the book Sacajawea

The Sacred Tree comes from the Book "The Sacred Tree"by the Four World's Development Project

Appendix

From Chapter 5 of 'Alita's Journey to Truth—The Early Years'

Alita's First Sweat

A few pages from the personal diary of Alita at the age of 21 years old, and later, sections were modified to be published in a local Native newspaper

Alphonse Peters Sr. (Punchy)

I write this in appreciation of Alphonse Peters Sr. who stated that it would be good for the People to hear of my experience in the Sweat. These pages are created out of respect and honor of this gentle, wise teacher and Spiritual Leader of the Sweat and the Sta'tli'imx Gathering of the Chiefs in May, 1998 at Portage Farm, Samahquam First Nation.

Dear Diary:

One of my primary reasons for coming to this gathering of 300 Natives was my strong desire to experience my first sweat. Shortly after my arrival, Red Owl asked if I would be participating in the sweat. Then Charlie Peters Sr. asked and I nodded a yes. By this time I was truly looking forward to the sweat, which was to begin at six in the morning.

The next morning wakening up at 5:45 a.m., I walked over to the sweat location, which was situated in a forested area to the right of the gathering. The helper, Brent, had just ignited the logs, which surrounded and topped the many Lava rocks. He had personally walked down from the Mountain carrying the lava rocks in his shirt, a shirt which had become full of holes by the end of the walk. There were a few giggles on how *holy* the shirt had become. I can only imagine how many trips he made.

I returned to my tent, put on my shorts and by 6:45 a.m. I returned to the sweat location. By now the rocks were red hot. I was in a peaceful state of mind, and felt protected by Alphonse and the other beautiful people of the sweat—nine of us together; 2 women and 7 men.

The sweat lodge was in the shape of a dome, approximately 7 or 8 feet across. Branches had been intertwined, establishing a foundation for the roof which was covered with blankets and tarps. The floor was dirt, with pieces of carpet on it for the people to sit on—mostly cross legged. In the middle, was a fair size pit for the lava rocks. Everyone brought a towel and wore shorts.

So, in I crawled and this was my experience of my first sweat.

Round 1

I found my spot next to Alphonse and Linda. Alphonse began the sweat by quietly talking about the Creator. He mentioned that his was the way of 7 rocks, others might have 4, but this was his way that was taught to him by the People of the midlands of USA, Sioux I believe. Linda mentioned to me that there is no right or wrong way.

Roy, being the Watchman, sat outside the Sweat Lodge lifting one rock at a time out of the fire with a pitchfork and carried it into the pit. When a big rock appeared, there was excitement and talk that it must be the Grandfather. All rocks are good Grandfathers/Grandmothers. After bringing in the required number of rocks, Roy asked permission to say a few words about the Creator, The Spirits and the sweat. Then, he pulled the tarp over the door and it became pitch black, except for the rocks. My eyes had no problem adjusting.

Smudge, in the form of tobacco, was laid on the rocks and it glowed and smelled nice. Alphonse talked about the Creator for a few moments. Then, he dipped a cedar bough into the water bucket which had some ground up lavender for healing in it, and swatted it over the rocks.

I was in a peaceful state of mind. I intuitively knew that I could not figure this experience out. I did not have any idea what was coming, so I did what I understood to be the wisest approach— I quieted my mind of its thoughts, and experienced the sweat with a free, open mind, for I knew I was stepping into the *unknown*. The hand drummer began his drumming and song, it was beautifully soothing. I heard the words of the song kind of blurred like, but I was listening. The first round was the longest and quite hot—it felt like a purification, whereby I relaxed and became comfortable and free with the sweat. The door finally opened and we all slowly crawled out into the fresh air, surrounded by the magnificence of the forest. I liked what I experienced and felt totally part of the group. We talked casually while our skins and the inside of our noses cooled.

Round 2

Everyone re-entered on their knees and made their way back to their same spots. Another 7 rocks, which were sitting in the fire outside of the lodge, were gently and carefully piled onto the original 7 in the pit. Roy asked to talk again, stating he felt the Spirits all around and they were powerful. He then closed the door again, leaving no light to shine through.

Alphonse talked in a wise way how we are a poor People, as this allows us to be humble and that humility is a great strength in the eyes of the Creator. He talked about promises not being good as they often have disappointed the People. He gave some beautiful common sense tips about the Creator.

Alphonse shook water on the rocks and the heat increased. The moaning, *releases of emotions*, and singing by the others were much stronger and strangely soothing. While others experienced flying, and had their emotions all over the sweat, I became calmer and felt an outpouring of personal sighs. Some negative thought patterns about my two closest friends released within me. I found that I had been attached in a negative way to these thoughts and recognized that the answer lay in forgiveness, rather than being right. This round was definitely deeper for me.

Alphonse asked each member of the sweat to talk. Each talk was incredibly beautiful, sensitive and spiritual. Many were about the freeing and forgiveness from their own destructive thoughts; and one's connection to the almighty Creator. My turn came, and a comfortable feeling flowed into me.

'I thanked the Creator for sending such gentle teachers in my first sweat, for I truly needed their gentle guidance into something, which I knew almost nothing about. Responses from Alphonse and the rest were feelings of appreciation.

'I asked the Creator to send the necessary love and understanding to provide healing for the People. And to alleviate the suffering of the People which was so small in comparison to the Beauty of the Creator". Again, responses from Alphonse and the rest were of appreciation.

In Round 1, when Mike began singing an Indian prayer and hand drummed, I found this soothing and pleasant. In Round 2, my mind quieted, I started to hear the words and beat of the song and hummed along. I was entering a deeper state of meditation. That felt good. I experienced the value of a song—it embraces our mind, distracting it off the sweat and drawing it closer to the Spirit.

The round ended with Alphonse saying *"All my Relations"*. I crawled out again into the cool air. This time I only stayed for a few seconds to clear out my lungs and take some deep breaths. One of the young members, who had remained inside the sweat, was singing religious and spiritual songs that were a glorious outpouring of his soul—his singing gently, but powerfully filled the nature around us.

Another of the members of the sweat felt complete with his experience, and flowed back to the gathering. Also, Alphonse had experienced some physical discomfort, so another member from Lillooet would head the remaining rounds of the sweat.

Round 3

Another 7 red-hot rocks were gently and carefully piled on the original 14 rocks. Roy asked to talk again, saying he usually did not talk like this until Round 4, but the Spirits were very powerful and had entered the Lodge, and that there was great healing taking place.

I immediately felt comfortable with the new Sweat Lodge Holder. He openly acknowledged that Alphonse was the Spiritual leader of the sweat and I liked this calm leadership. Mike began the drumming and a new song, and this time I started to sing along, quietly. My confidence soared as I was flowing into this ceremony gracefully and with enthrallment.

This round was highlighted by stronger sighs, moans and releases of energy by the others. I was really getting into it. I was feeling extremely close to Linda, who was cuddled next to me. This had an interesting positive side effect. I had spent some past time with her, and had developed some foolish, preconceived ideas about her limited psychological understanding. This had blinded me to her beauty and wisdom. Somehow, when one shares a Sweat, it is almost like all the members are traveling on a solitary ship, whose name is love and compassion.

My experience was deepening. Round 1 was identified with purification; Round 2 with negative thoughts and our personal relationship with the Creator. Round 3 was about opening up to the Creator and allowing *my spiritual feelings to freely fly out.*

Somehow, I had deliberately developed a coping or control mechanism, which had strangled or created a film over my feelings, and which, I falsely felt protected me. This coping thought had prevented my positive, spiritual feelings from escaping or flowing freely. The time had come for me to let go of this thought, and to once again be my natural self—much like a child does naturally. I instinctively knew this was true, and I felt like I was in the womb of the Mother and she was saying—Feeeeel life and your feelings will bring life to the essence of your being.

Suddenly Round 3 was over as someone shouted '*All my Relations*', which meant they wanted out. This time, I remained in the cocoon of the Mother, while others went out for fresh air. I had been cooked, the rocks and the water from the cedar boughs had provided major heat, but I was not uncomfortable. I was definitely super relaxed and smiling.

Round 4

The others re-entered the sweat lodge. Roy piled another 7 rocks with a pitchfork onto the original 7 + 14. This time it was even hotter, but I liked it. There was more moaning and singing. The drummer and his song were crystal clear, and I freely sang. I loved the singing, it was freeing. People were being healed, so was I. I experienced something very simple and beautiful.

MY EXPERIENCE—I could feel an inner force pushing up from the top of my head and originating from the middle of my being. It was almost like a small, tight cylinder, and I could feel my resistance at the top, as this force gently and very slowly kept rising. These blockages were my fears, insecurities and my inability to let go of my feelings in the past. They were not bad things, they were simply life and what every human being has. I was no different, except now I was being freed from many of them—what I would call many of my bad habits of thought. I did not feel ecstasy, I felt calm and being helped by the Creator to push away my Fears.

Round 4 ended with another Member saying All My Relations, and most crawled out of the Lodge. This time I crawled out too, not because I wanted to, but my leg had developed a major cramp. After vigorously rubbing it, the cramp went away.

Bonus Round

To my surprise, there was another round. I was pleased but I knew I had very little inner strength left in me. I knew it would be my turn to say All My Relations. I crawled back in and now there were only 4 of us left.

More rocks were brought in. Brent said to me that this round would be short but sweet and I acknowledged that I didn't have much left anyway. He suggested that I lie down for this round and I did.

I don't know what they did to the rocks as I was lying down, but boy!!!! did it start to get hot. The bottom of my feet started to really heat up. My chest started to burn up and I took it for as long as I could. One of the members was singing a song, so I started to sing his song to get my mind off the heat. But the Sweat Lodge Holder gently slapped me on my leg with the bough and I took this as a sign that this was not good.

Finally, the heat became too much, and as I was burning up, I yelled '*All My Relations*'. One of the members said to crawl out slowly, but these were unfollowed words, as I was moving quickly. *I made it* out into the air, and lay in the dirt, with sweat all over me. I was mellllow and empty. I was smiling and felt great, but I could not move for at least 20 minutes. I talked with members as they were dressing and leaving. Finally, I slowly arose and walked along the path.

I met the youngest member of the Sweat, with the holy songs and voice. He mentioned he had taken a quick swim in the glacial lake. I slowly strolled down to the lake (anything beyond a slow stroll was out of the question), and looked all around. The mountain to the left was called the In-SHUCK-ch Mountain, and it had snow on the top and the sun shining over it. The mountain on the left was treed and the lake in front of me was majestic. I walked into the lake, as quick as possible, then dove head first. This was instantly followed by the biggggest *YELP* anyone has ever heard. It was glacier cold and freezing, and I ran out dramatically. It was totally refreshing, and I was clean and alive, but there was no way I was going in there again. Many of the members of the gathering laughed spontaneously as they heard my yelp, even though they were a distance away. I felt like I belonged.

The Rest of the Day

I enjoyed the gathering for the remainder of the day. I was mellow and felt elevated. The love, respect and peaceful feelings of the gathering touched my heart. My feelings were heavenly. The People had become relaxed and content, and there was no talk about politics or complaints. This set a healing and optimistic tone for the 10 Chiefs and the People at the gathering.

From Chapter 6

The Final Episode of Alita's First Sweat
—Sharing—

The Next Morning and a Different Kind of Sweat

I had heard the next sweat would be in the evening, after the gathering. Because of this assumption, I partied in front of a roaring fire with 8 good-natured teenagers, and an Elder until 2:30 in the morning. The Elder's job was to be awake all night, and guarantee the eternal fire did not die out before the Gathering finished. It was a fun loving party, an evening of lighthearted jokes and riddles, amusing conversation and no alcohol. When I awoke the next morning, I was surprised to hear that a sweat was in progress. Interestingly, I was not disappointed. I instinctively recognized that I was not ready for another full sweat.

Around 8:00 a.m., my curiosity got the better of me and I decided to drift over to the sweat. Alphonse was walking down the path from the sweat lodge, and I casually mentioned that I had been misinformed about the time of the sweat. He gently mentioned that the Lodge was empty and that if I felt like it, I could go in by myself. He quietly encouraged me. NOW, that felt perfect—a private time with the Creator, for as short or long as I needed. I eagerly walked to the lodge, and mentioned to a sweat member what Alphonse had suggested. He pointed to the rocks in the smoldering fire, and asked if I wanted to take them into the sweat myself, and I nodded my head affirmatively.

Nearby, Brent mentioned that I should do this very carefully and gently, as they were the Grandfather of the People. I respected his guidance, as always. The hand drummer mentioned *quite seriously* to be careful to place the rocks on the correct side. I thought for a second, and then he smiled and roared into laughter. We laughed heartily together, with myself giggling and acknowledging that I had been totally fooled by his wit.

A few minutes later, I cautiously began to pile 5 individual large red-hot rocks from the smoldering fire onto the cooled rocks inside the sweat lodge. One was enormous, and as I gathered it on the pitchfork, suddenly realized to my dismay, the larger the rock, the stronger the heat—but since it was already on my pitchfork, I carried the Grandfather of all Grandfather rocks into the pit.

Then, I crawled in and closed the entrance. The heat was intense as I still felt 'cooked' from yesterday. YES, those big rocks sure gave off heat. I sat and melted, beginning to sing a gentle prayer about life, truth and the Mother. I loved the intimate atmosphere of being alone. As I sang a song of unstructured prayer to the Mother, my relationship with Her became clearer. This is what was revealed: *The Mother was being very gentle, nurturing and full of warm, tender feelings, as I metaphorically swam in these safe feelings as they encompassed my entire being.* My respect for the female side of life grew appreciatively. *Safe feelings guide humans, allowing them to feel whole and real. Our connection to the Creator comes through our sacred relationship with the Mother, and our ability to feel via the five senses.* I permeated in this soft-flowing feeling of tenderness, protection and compassion for over twenty minutes.

Then, my mind and song causally moved over to the Father. What an immense and immediate **CHANGE**. *I could sense the almighty strength and fire of the Father. This god-like Power and Wisdom commanded instant respect and obedience. A sense of vulnerability, fear and awe overpowered my consciousness, much like an average high school athlete might experience if she was asked to represent her country in the Olympics. I felt minuscule compared to the omnipotent Power of the Father. After continuing to sing my inward song for a few heart-stopping moments, I acknowledged it was enough.* I quietly and humbly crawled out, thanking the Grandfathers and the Mother for their immense guidance. I had loved being alone in the HOLY SWEAT LODGE and having a personal conversation with the Creator.

I felt complete with my first sweat experience, and strolled back to the gathering. My connection to the People, the Creator and my understanding of Native Spirituality had dramatically deepened. In fact it was one of the most beautiful experiences of my life. I HIGHLY RECOMMEND IT. ...